A CHRISTMAS CACTUS FOR THE GENERAL

IMP Universe

ANGEL MARTINEZ

Edited by

ERIKA ORRICK

COPYRIGHT

About the Book You Have Purchased:

This copy is intended for the original purchaser of this book ONLY. No part of this book may be reproduced, scanned, or distributed in any printed or electronic form without prior written permission from the authors. Please do not participate in or encourage piracy of copyrighted materials in violation of the author's rights. Purchase only authorized editions.

Cover Artist: Freddy MacKay
Editor: Erika Orrick

First Edition
A Christmas Cactus for the General © 2014 Angel Martinez
All Rights Reserved.
Published in the United States of America.

ALL RIGHTS RESERVED: *A Christmas Cactus for the General* is a work of fiction. Names, places, characters, and incidents are either the product of the author's imagination or are fictionalized. Any resemblance to any actual persons, living or dead, is entirely coincidental. The story contains explicit sexual content and is intended for adult readers.

Any person depicted in the Licensed Art Material is a model and is being used solely for illustrative purposes.

PUBLISHER
Mischief Corner Books, LLC

CONTENTS

TRADEMARKS ACKNOWLEDGEMENT

The author acknowledges the trademarked status and trademark owners of the following word marks mentioned in this work of fiction:

Crock-Pot: Sunbeam Products, Inc.
KFC: KFC Corporation
Mario: Nintendo of America Inc.
Sleep Number: Select Comfort Corporation

CHAPTER ONE

Exile

So much water. General Teer checked the boards again, but he had read his instruments correctly. In the entire vast universe, there were bound to be planets such as this one, but his Irasolan brain refused to accept it. *So much water.*

Granted, much of it was saline, but those huge salt-laden expanses drove weather patterns. There would be rain more than once every few years. Enough rain that plants grew on the surface, *huge* plants in some cases, the likes of which he could not have imagined in dreams.

Oxygen levels ran a bit high, the average temperature too warm for comfort. *I have only two choices remaining, though: acclimate or die. Perhaps it would be better...*

No. His Exalted Keeropness had taken that from him. Denied an honorable execution and sent into exile, his last shred of honor would burn in the winds of this alien sun if he took his life now. No one would know, of course. Still, the idea was too repugnant to entertain for more than a moment.

Teer tapped into the record pod to send his final message home. "I, General Teer of the Second Horath, hero of the Violet Day Offensive, acknowledge my arrival in orbit around the planet of exile. I confirm that I have no knowledge of this system's coordinates. My stasis sleep remained uninterrupted throughout transit. I failed you, Karet. For that, I am deeply sorry. For the good of the people and the Keerop, I resign myself to this uncharted gravity well. May the mother of seeds have mercy on me."

With a sharp hiss, the landing pod closed around him, molding to his body so tightly he felt he would suffocate until the inner membrane began to feed him oxygen in little sips, just enough to keep him alive. The edges of his vision darkened. It was better to make these pod flights half-conscious.

The words of an old spacer's prayer whispered in his head as the pod launched. *I step out of the great night into the unknown. May the gravity pit's clutching embrace leave me breath and bone.*

FOR THE FIRST WEEK, TEER HID. THE DOMINANT bipedal species built cities and obviously had global communications tech, but he knew precious little else about them since the comm system on the exile drone had limited applications. He lurked in filthy access ways between buildings, trying to glean enough words for the translation chip in his brain, watching these strange beings with little shivers of revulsion.

They covered their bodies but left their naked faces exposed, a practice Teer found obscene. One didn't parade around with a naked face. It was so uncivilized. There did appear to be two genders. At least that was familiar. But with a nearly equal number of each, how did one tell the males from the females? He thought he had it after enough observation. The often smaller ones, the ones with more elegant noses and body structures, he thought must be the males. Many of them walked successfully on complex, heel-elevated shoes, much more graceful than the shambling, larger ones. These, he reasoned, were the ones fit for battle. The larger ones seemed likely to fall on their faces in close combat.

Projecting his cultural biases was dangerous. He understood that but needed to cling to something for the sake of sanity, something that nearly came unhinged one night when he observed a mating pair through an unsecured window.

They were nearly hairless, both genders. That was horrid enough. The larger one had some sort of *external* genitalia. From what Teer could tell, none of it had descended during mating. It appeared permanently external. It seemed both a biologically dangerous way to carry an ovipositor and an odd placement for one, at the apex of the thighs. He didn't see any way that the smaller one would be able to deposit fertilization gametes either. The big one simply thrust the ovipositor into the smaller one. Perhaps all of the male organs were internal. At least that would come close to sensible adaptation.

Afterward, he was too nauseous and ashamed to go to his usual refuse container to scavenge for discarded meat. At least he wasn't in danger of starving, but there had to be a reason why the people of this planet threw away so much food. Perhaps they had some biological recycling he had yet to encounter.

At the start of the second week, his language acquisition accelerated to the point where he felt he could communicate. By this time, he had also found a public container of discarded clothing to cover his pelt. Since no other builder species inhabited the planet, assimilation would be vital. For all he knew, he might be their first offworld person, and those sorts of contacts tended to end badly.

He found a bright pink and blue shirt with a high collar and a pair of the blue leggings they called "pants" that didn't offend his sense of harmony too badly, plus a pair of gloves to cover his furred hands and a pair of boots with moderate heels. More than likely, being unable to walk in the challenging footwear would be seen as a sign of weakness. He would need to learn. His mane had grown out enough to cover his ears that were different enough to cause alarm. That left only his furless neck and face exposed, to his everlasting shame. He had spotted two or three humans wearing something similar to the *kurya* to cover their heads and faces, but those were so few, it was most likely a sign of status.

Best to blend in with the common ones.

Head high, only wobbling every few steps, Teer made his way to what he understood was a resettlement assistance facility. "Homeless shelter" was an odd thing to call it, since the shelter didn't require a home, but he wasn't going to quibble over semantics. He would find some way to contribute in this alien society and access their credit system. From there, it was only a matter of time before he acquired a den of his own and perhaps some resurrected serenity.

CHAPTER TWO

That Weird Little Man at Benson's

"TGIF, huh, Bruce?" Hal, the new mechanic, shot him a grin and a too-cheery wave on his way into the office.

"What the fuck ever," Bruce snarled, shouldering his way out the door. He'd just landed his last scheduled flight of stupid hunters for the week. One last nerve, he didn't have.

"Shh, Hal," Belinda said from behind the reception desk. "We don't say that to him."

"Why not? What's his problem?"

The explanation, if Belinda gave one, cut off as the door snicked shut. Quiet. Blessed, blessed quiet. He needed that more than anything else. Some weeks, Fridays weren't that bad anymore. A little melancholy, but bearable. During the run-up to the holidays, though, they started to suck big brass donkey balls again.

He shrugged into his sheepskin coat and trudged through the loose-packed snow to his truck. Some Novembers brought a ton of the white stuff. Others, not so much. So far, there'd only been about eight inches total for the month, not enough to slow down any self-respecting Alaskan. Certainly not enough to keep him from his regular Friday routine.

Same route, same set of steps every Friday. He wasn't sure if it was superstition or some fucked-up way to seek comfort from something familiar. First stop was for the takeout order of Kung Pao chicken from the Fly In restaurant. Belinda always called it in for him when he radioed he was landing. It was always ready for him by the time he got there.

Next stop was Benson's as he headed north. Maybe it wasn't the biggest florist nearby, but he'd always stopped there, so he didn't change it. He didn't want to change anything. Unexpected things aggravated him during his Friday trip, so it pissed him off when Molly had hired that new guy to help in the shop.

Pissed him off something fierce.

Bruce parked the truck and stomped into the shop, already irritated that the little twit was behind the counter.

"The same as last week, sir?" The soft voice didn't quite lisp, but it might as well have.

"Yeah, the same. It's always the same." Bruce tapped his fingers on the counter, scowling as this... this thing minced into the back to get his regular order. *At least his fucking heels aren't as high today.*

He came back with the purchase impeccably wrapped, a single, purple hyacinth, shook his hair back so the damn hoops in his left ear jingled, and said, "Was there anything else, sir?"

That was it. Bruce's last nerve. "No, there's not any fucking thing else! There's never anything else! Do you want to take my goddamned money or not, you little twink shit?"

The shouting brought Molly racing out from the back room. "Bruce! Stop bellowing. What in the world's the matter?"

Chest heaving, face heated almost to sweating, Bruce snarled, "He asked if there was anything else."

Molly came around the counter and took his arm to lead him a few steps away. "That's what he's supposed to do. You have a problem with Teer?"

"Teer? What the hell kind of a name is that? And yeah, I've got a fucking problem. Him and his heels and his bright parrot clothes and his soft little voice! Girly little faggots like that give the rest of us a bad name! Why can't he man up a little? Why does he have to try so damn hard to be all queenie?"

She patted his chest. "I'm pretty sure you're upset about something else, so I'm not tossing you out this time. Teer's not from around here. I think he's Thai or something. They do things different over there. He works hard, he's got an incredible eye for flowers, and he's never late, so don't pick on him, okay? He's just who he is."

When he managed a curt nod, Molly took his money and brought him change while he stood by the door. The little twerp watched him the whole time, no expression on his elfin-magic little face.

His mood and his routine fouled by the incident, Bruce stomped out, muttering, "Fucking pansy."

Teer kept still, watching the man drive off. The men on this world amazed him, such clumsy, uncontrolled louts, like overgrown children. If that had been one of his own men back home, Mr. Bruce would have been on the floor with a boot against his windpipe. But Teer couldn't do such things here. It was, from what he understood, illegal.

"A pansy seems an honorable flower. Such strong colors," he said as Molly returned to him. "But I'm fairly certain that wasn't a compliment."

"No, it wasn't." Molly pursed her lips, an expression Teer knew by now meant she was unhappy. "I'm sorry about that. I think he goes to visit someone in the cemetery every Friday. But it's no excuse to act like a son of a bitch."

Sometimes it still struck Teer as odd, working for a female, but Molly was a sensible, practical person, more like a male Irasolan than most of the men on this strange, wet planet.

"When you say he visits someone at the cemetery, is this a way of saying he goes to honor someone who has died?"

Molly gave him an odd look, then shook her head. "I'm sorry. Your English is so good, I forget you get tripped up by expressions sometimes. Yeah. I'm pretty sure he lost someone close to him."

The single hyacinth every week seemed an extravagant tribute, but Teer had to tamp down hard on his instincts every time he filled a customer's order. Flowers to these people were *disposable*, things of temporary beauty that could be callously cut from their parent plants. A single plant given to the honored dead back home would have been a sign of such overarching grief that the survivor's family would have feared an imminent suicide attempt.

But for this man, the tribute paid is every week. His wounds are deep, but not fatal. Not that I have any reason to be curious or even vaguely interested. Rude, uncouth...what is the word? Jerk.

"Ah. Never fear, Molly. It's difficult to be offended by words that don't mean much to me." He offered her a smile, since smiles were often meant as reassurance here. "You said you had lights to put up today? For the upcoming holidays?"

"Right! The Christmas lights!" Molly scurried to the back and returned with two boxes full of small glass bulbs attached to wires. "I guess you don't do Christmas either, huh?"

"My...family never celebrated Christmas, no."

"Oh, right. Buddhist or something, I bet."

"Something of that sort," Teer murmured as he began to pull one of the hopelessly tangled strands from the first box. Apparently, Christmas had something to do with testing spatial acuity and patience. Odd holiday.

Anchorage Memorial was beautiful in the snow, all the trees dressed in white diamonds. Since most of the markers here were ground-level ones, it always gave Bruce the impression that someone had spread a blanket over the graves to keep them safe and hidden until spring. Not that he needed to see where he was going. He could do this walk even if the sun burned out. Past the chokecherry tree, past the whale jawbone sculpture, he knew the direction and the precise number of steps even in four feet of snow.

When he reached the spot, he dropped to one knee and swept away the inch or so of snow that had fallen the night before.

MIKE SPECTOR 1979-2012

"HEY, BOWSER. HOW'VE YOU BEEN?" THE SNOW wasn't too deep and he didn't care if his ass got wet, so Bruce plunked down in front of the marker, placing the hyacinth carefully to the left of Mike's name. "You would've laughed your ass off today, swear to god. Had a pickup this afternoon, nasty landing. Everything froze about a week ago, so we're on straight skis already. Hit a patch of mud coming in. So already I'm worried about takeoff, right? And these idiots, two of them, they wanted to load three moose on to my plane. *Three*."

Bruce shook his head on a caustic laugh. "I told them, 'Boys, you're gonna have to choose. I can take two of you and maybe two moose, one if I don't like the feel of takeoff. Or I can take the three moose and leave you here.' Oh hell yeah, they fussed and cussed, but I wasn't gonna pull some bonehead move just 'cause the customer's always right. It was moose, damn it, not some medical emer—"

The sun was sinking into one of the pine trees across the cemetery, blood red light running down the trunk. Bruce swallowed hard, fighting the memories. They weren't as bad anymore, not most days.

"Thanksgiving next week, Mike. I'll probably eat out again somewhere. I know you'd yell at me. But it's hard, you know. It's just so damn hard." He ran a gloved finger down the edge of the *M*, sharing the snow-covered quiet with Mike for a few minutes. Finally, he stood and brushed the snow off his numb ass. "Almost closing time. I better get going before they toss me out. Be back next week. Promise."

Sure it was stupid, talking to a headstone. It wasn't as if Mike could hear him. But it was that last connection, the one he was afraid to let go. If he let go of this, Mike would slip away into those dark waters forever and he'd never get him back, not even in his dreams.

CHAPTER THREE

Schlumbergera

Teer tugged at the cuffs of his work gloves, the ones Molly assumed he wore for reasons of vanity. How she would react to the fur covering his hands, he couldn't predict. It wasn't worth the risk. But he was often overheated and uncomfortable indoors, since the peltless humans preferred things warmer and he overdressed to hide his fur. At least the outdoor temperatures in this city were gradually decreasing to something livable.

"Did you have a nice Thanksgiving?" Molly called from the back. They were, once again, the only employees in the store since the young ones who worked shorter hours would not be in that day.

"It was a quiet day."

"Oh, Teer, don't tell me you spent the whole day alone?"

He turned to lean in the doorway to the back room where they constructed elaborate arrangements of flowers. "I understood that this holiday was for families." *In addition to the mass consumption of ungainly domesticated avians and otherwise engaging in an orgy of overeating.*

"It's not just for families. You should've told me you didn't have plans. You could've come to our house." Molly added sprigs of baby's breath to a spectacular grouping of scarlet roses, the delicacy of her task halting her scolding for a brief, blissful moment. Naturally, she wasn't finished with him. "I worry about you sometimes, you know? You never talk about friends or going out. Do you go home every night and stare at the walls?"

"I have a television and a tablet now for...surfing."

"Uh-huh. You probably don't even watch porn, do you?"

"Porn?" He should have simply researched the term later based on the incredulous look Molly shot him.

"You probably call it something else. Movies of people having sex?"

For others to watch? How...dreadful. Are they coerced? Is it filmed secretly? Or perhaps it's nonprofessional playacting, what are they called...reality shows? "Oh...yes. That is, no! No, I don't watch those."

Molly straightened from the worktable, frowning. "You can't just be alone all the time, Teer. I mean, this is Anchorage, not some little town on the ass end of nowhere. We do have gay bars and stuff. For Christ's sake, go out and meet people. Go to Mad Myrna's for a show. Go to a bar if you don't like the clubs. I hate to think of you sitting at home every night like some loser geek who still lives with his mom." She stopped and narrowed her eyes. "You don't live with your mom, do you?"

"Ah, no. I'm a bit past that age."

"Right. No family here. Sorry. But you're young. You're gorgeous. Go out and have some fun, damn it."

This seemed to go beyond Molly's usual teasing. Some species failed to thrive in socially deprived circumstances. He hadn't observed that humans were one of those species, perhaps because they lived so tightly packed together.

"I will, Molly. I'm doing my best to get used to things here."

"Of course you are. I don't mean to harass you—"

The bell above the door chimed, saving him from further Molly interrogation. Teer turned back to the front of the shop and had to school his features carefully. It was Friday afternoon, so he should have expected Mr. Bruce.

"I'll bring it right out for you, sir," Teer offered, his tone calm and civilized as a matter of pride.

To his credit, Mr. Bruce only nodded, lips pressed in a thin line.

"Want me to get this?" Molly whispered as he wrapped the single hyacinth.

Teer's stomach fluttered in shame that she thought so little of him. *My dear employer, I faced down the fiercest ships in the Fara battle fleet, do you think I fear a single childish man?* "No, thank you."

The plastic and foil wrapped hyacinth was hardly his weapon of choice, but he had never shrunk from confrontation. Because of this and because he was feeling contrary, Teer set the purchase on the counter, raised his head to meet the human's eyes, and asked, "Will there be anything else?"

Mr. Bruce turned a shade of red to match Molly's

roses. "No. Thanks." He seemed to be chewing on the inside of his cheek. "Look. I'm sorry I was a jackass. I don't want you thinking everyone here's a bigot or anything."

Ah, perhaps he's a grown male, after all. He has the most interesting green eyes. Green, like sira *lichen.* "I accept your apology."

"I mean, you're probably one of those ladyboys or something, right?" Mr. Bruce ran a hand over the back of his neck, clearly uncomfortable. "Or, damn, you're trans, aren't you?"

"Trans?"

"You were born female, you know, biologically, but your brain says you're male. Or maybe the other way around with you. Damn it."

Teer opened his mouth, closed it again, and tried to process whether he was offended or simply confused. He had completed the sale and set the change on the counter before he could blurt out, "I assure you, I was born male and remain entirely male."

"Fuck, I'm screwing this all up. Look, I'm not some homophobic asshole. Not like I'm one of those guys too far in the closet to see who the fuck he is. I just—I mean, would it kill you to wear a flannel shirt sometimes and a pair of regular boots? The orange looks good on you, don't get me wrong, but do you have to try so damn hard to be in your face?"

With his breathing carefully controlled—it wouldn't do to growl at a customer—Teer answered in the soft tone reserved for unhappy children, "Where I am from, males wear stronger colors. I am uncomfortable wearing the drab, weak colors many of the men here wear." *I'm uncomfortable wearing so many clothes in the first place, but you don't need to know that.*

Mr. Bruce picked up his purchase, as gentle and careful with it as all his other movements were brash and half-violent. "You're the strangest little man I've ever met."

"Perhaps that will always be the case." Teer nodded to the windows. "It will be dark soon."

"Yeah. Thanks," Mr. Bruce muttered, shaking his head as his stomped out.

Again, Teer stood stock-still as Mr. Bruce drove away. Human sexuality had more layers than a formal mating cloak, so complex that human nations had sexual *politics*, of all bizarre things. The notion of having different gender preferences for sex or even no preference at all was simply so...alien. An Irasolan male mated with females for breeding and picked a life partner from among his male peers. Females mated with males and chose life partners from among the females of their acquaintance. It really shouldn't have been so complicated, though he did understand that human biology played a large part, and perhaps having a greater ratio of females to males than one to every fifty was also a factor.

With a huff of breath, he got back to work, moving the pallets with the "Christmas stock" out to the front of the shop. The poinsettias had a special table cleared for them by the front window. Red, white, pink, and variegated, they were lovely. Molly said they grew wild in areas closer to the planet's equator. *What an incredible sight that must be.*

When he took the plastic cover off the second pallet, his heart gave a painful stuttering thump.

Schlumbergera—Christmas Cactus, the tags read, along with color designations—white, salmon, magenta, red, and yellow. An ache started deep in his chest. They looked uncannily like the treasured *alna* succulents back home. So elegant, so perfect. The sudden urge to howl in homesick misery nearly sucked him under.

"Teer? You okay?"

"I'm...yes. These reminded me of something. They're beautiful."

"Be even prettier when they start blooming in about a week. You want me to hold one back for you?"

Own an *alna*? He shook his head. Even though he knew they weren't those rare, prized plants, knew they probably grew by the dozens in some greenhouse on this planet, he wouldn't have felt right having one in his home. He was an exile, unworthy of such pretensions. "No, thank you. I don't really have a place for it right now."

"All right. Let me know if you change your mind."

Molly was giving him that odd look again, so he smiled and went back to placing plants on the tables. If he kept his back turned, she wouldn't be able to see his hands shaking.

One stupid holiday down, two to go. Bruce sat at the bar at Wesley's, ignoring the happy idiots all around him. A week after Thanksgiving, still three more weeks until Christmas, he was mortally tired of all the cheery greetings and the happy-ass holiday music. If he had to hear "Santa Baby" one more time in any commercial establishment, he was going to start ripping speakers out of the walls.

And I used to like Eartha Kitt.

This was the last part of his Friday ritual. The only reason he still drove to Wesley's to grab a drink or two before heading home was because Mike always had. Maybe it was time to cut this part back. But Mike always sat with him, talking a mile a minute to whoever would listen, the big, friendly bear. They called him Bowser because he was built like the bad guy in the Mario games, but the disposition never matched.

It was probably damn unhealthy, hanging on to Mike like this. He didn't give even half a rat's ass.

"Hey, BB gun!" A hand smacked him on the back a little too hard.

"Look, it's Bering Not-so-straight!"

Bruce spared a sideways glance at two of Wesley's regulars, Jake and Caleb. He had no clue what these clowns did for a living. For all he knew, they were professional barflies. "Yeah. Hey."

"So, listen to this one, BB." Caleb thumped him on the back again. "What do gay kids get for Christmas?"

Bruce ignored him, but Jake took the bait. "I dunno. What?"

"Erection Sets!"

"Hilarious," Bruce muttered into his beer.

"Oh, wait, how about this one? How do you fit three fags on one barstool?"

Bruce put his beer down. "Watch it."

"Turn it upside-down!"

Jake roared with laughter while Bruce turned on the barstool to face them. "I'm not laughing. You see me not laughing, right?"

"Aw, poor BB. All alone and missing his bu—"

That was as far as Caleb got with Bruce's hand around his throat. "Take it somewhere else, jackasses. This gay man isn't gonna simper and mince for you."

"Leave Bering alone, boys," the bartender interrupted. "Go back to your table or I'll have to cut you off."

"We were just messing around, Trent," Jake said hastily, but he had a hand on Caleb's arm, already dragging him away.

Every city probably had assholes. Anchorage was damn tolerant, but yeah, no way to escape the asshole factor, no matter where you lived.

Everyone knew about him and Mike, but people had always left them alone. Bruce was taller than most of the guys he knew by a good couple of inches, not all gym-rat buff, but still big. Mike had been bigger.

Together they could've—damn it. Bruce slammed down the rest of his beer and ordered a second. Definitely a two-beer night. He leaned his elbow on the bar top, second mug in hand, and watched the crowd, trying to get his back muscles to unwind. The buzz of conversation, the ebb and flow of people moving around the room was almost soothing. Tables gained and lost people or changed hands entirely. Patrons table-hopped and stopped to say hello where they recognized a face. The crowd thinned toward the back for a moment, and he caught a glint of bright orange.

Oh hell no.

Tucked into the corner seat of the back table, a familiar figure sat ramrod straight, his dark eyes staring around the room, his gloved—*gloved?*—hands tracing lines on his glass. Teer.

"Just stay back there. Don't let those assholes see you," Bruce muttered. Not that he gave a shit what happened to the little freak. Why would he? Well, beyond being a decent human being and not wanting to see someone get the shit kicked out of him.

The little guy didn't seem to be cruising, though. He just sat there and watched. Maybe he was waiting for someone. Bruce relaxed and went back to his beer. A couple more minutes and he'd be heading home anyway, another long week over. He kept waiting for them to get more bearable, for the nights to feel less like liquid despair, but after two years, it hadn't happened yet.

After another few sips, an orange flicker caught Bruce's eye. He turned to see Teer making his way toward the door. *Good. Calling it an early night.* His relief evaporated when five patrons, including Jake and Caleb, followed Teer out not twenty seconds later.

"Aw, crap." Bruce plunked his mug on the bar, fumbled out a couple of bills, threw on his coat, and hurried outside.

No Teer, no band of jackasses. For a long moment, Bruce stood balanced on the balls of his feet, tense and alert. Then Teer's impossibly soft voice drifted out of the alley beside the bar, his words unintelligible but even and calm. The voices answering him weren't. Menacing and angry, the other voices got louder every time Teer answered in his calm, reasonable way. He heard the words *fucking queer* and *flaming faggot* loud and clear, though.

Bruce raced toward the alley, praying he wouldn't be too late. He'd make those assholes pay for picking on someone half their size either way. One of the bigger ones had Teer in a headlock. Caleb, that shit, pulled his fist back and gut-punched Teer. Teer grunted, but stayed mostly upright. Bruce had to give the little man credit.

All set to barrel in to the rescue, he skidded to a stop when Teer reached up and grabbed his captor's arms. The man screamed, blood running down to his elbows as he staggered back. Knives? Broken glass? What had Teer pulled and from where?

The bleeding man tried to stagger back from him, but Teer seized one of his wrists, shifted his weight, and hurled that man over his shoulder to slam him into the concrete. The second, probably full up on liquid courage, charged him and got a boot heel to the throat when Teer spun and kicked impossibly high. A third guy ran up behind Teer and slammed a bottle over his head. The shivering splinter of glass nearly stopped Bruce's heart. He had to get to the end of this damn alley. Why was it so long?

Teer shook his head once and swung with a gloved fist, connecting with the side of bottle-man's head without looking. That asshole went down. Teer was still standing. Caleb and Jake no longer looked at all sure of themselves, and Bruce slowed his steps, shoving Jake out of the way so he could stand by Teer.

"Gentlemen, while the exercise was welcome, I don't think you have the training to offer any true sport," Teer said softly. He wasn't even breathing hard. "Shall we have a...what's the word? A ceasefire?"

"Sounds like sense to me," Bruce growled. "You boys are outgunned and outclassed."

"Not by you, Bering," Caleb said, his bravado ruined by his shaking voice. Still, he managed to pull some brain cells together, grabbed Jake, and left in a hurry.

Teer sighed, gazing around at his unconscious opponents. "I will be arrested now, I suppose."

"What? What for?"

"Assault, yes? I have done that here?"

"Oh fuck no. You defended yourself. They don't arrest you for that here."

"Ah. Good." Teer put a hand to the side of his head. "I don't think I would manage the walk to the police station."

"He got you good, that fucker." Bruce brushed a few shards of glass from Teer's head. "I should get you to the hospital."

"No!" For a split second, Teer's dark, teardrop eyes were wild and distressed. Then his usual calm mask slammed into place. "No. Thank you. No hospital. I...I want to go home."

Bruce couldn't be sure, but there might have been the tiniest hitch at the end of his sentence. "Is it far? Your place? At least let me walk you there. I'm not sure you'll make it."

"No. That is, yes." Teer rubbed his head again and swayed forward a step. "It's not far. I would appreciate the company of someone I know."

Apparently, Teer had been using the alley as a shortcut home since he continued through away from the bar and turned left. Bruce paced next to him, ready to catch him if he stumbled, but he made it to the door to his apartment building, not half a block away, without an uneven step.

"Wow. You are close. Guess it makes sense, you living here on the north side."

"The people who helped me find quarters said I would be happier here."

"Well, yeah, 'cause you're gay."

Teer gave him an odd look, part dazed exhaustion, part who the hell knew what else. "Yes. Yes, that. Good night, Mr. Bruce."

"It's not Mr. Bruce. Makes me sound like a damn plantation owner or something. You either call me Bruce or Mr. Bering if you need to be all formal." Bruce nodded at the building. "And no fucking way do I let you off the hook that easy. I'm coming up to get that head wound cleaned out and make sure you're all right."

"It's not necessary."

"The hell it isn't. You don't even have the sense to come out with a coat."

Teer let out a slow breath and started up the steps, though he didn't protest Bruce's tagging along. He got to the third floor, walked to the second door on the right, and stood there staring at it.

"Even the sky is the wrong color," he whispered.

Bruce nudged him, worried that he really did need the ER. "Hey? Key? Let's get you inside, okay?"

Gloved fingers shaking, Teer fumbled a key out of the pocket of his painted-on coffee-colored skinny jeans. How he fit anything in his pockets was a mystery. For a moment, he leaned his forehead against the door, then seemed to remember that he had to turn the knob before he could go in.

He whispered in some language Bruce couldn't identify, nothing he'd heard when he'd been stationed in South Korea as a Navy pilot. It wasn't Thai or Mandarin or even Vietnamese, as far as he could tell. Maybe one of the more rare Khmer dialects. Not that he gave a good goddamn. The issue now was that Teer was mumbling to himself, regardless of language, and wandering in dazed circles on his living room rug.

Living room was probably overstating the case. It was one of those small apartments with the front room and tiny galley kitchen in the same space. The room had two doors, most likely bedroom and bathroom. Not weird at all for someone who lived alone and probably made little more than minimum wage. Teer kept it neat. But there was something sad about the bare walls and the nonexistent clutter. He had a small flat-screen, a low, square table, the kind you'd find at nice Asian restaurants, with some floor cushions around it, and a single bright blue vase on the table. That was it, no canisters or appliances on the kitchen counter, no magazines, or CD racks. Nothing.

"Hey...hey, stop. Maybe sit down."

Bruce took hold of Teer to try to guide him to the cushions, but Teer wrenched his arm away with a snarl, a real animal snarl. No one should've been able to make that sound. Teer staggered two steps away and fell to his knees, clutching his head and making an odd fluttering sound in his throat reminiscent of a mourning dove's call on takeoff.

How much weirder can the little guy get? Bruce shook his head and stepped over to the kitchen, opening cabinets until he found a roll of paper towels. He took a couple of wet paper towels back to Teer and went down on one knee in front of him, pretty sure he was about to get slugged since Teer obviously wasn't tracking.

"We're gonna start with your gloves, okay? Whatever you did in that alley got the fingers all ripped and bloody. Need to check if any of it's yours."

Teer was muttering to himself again, maybe angry muttering, but it was hard to tell. Gently, Bruce took hold of the glove on his right hand and tugged. *Why does he have on another pair of—oh holy fucking hells.*

With the ruined glove still in his hand, Bruce sat down hard. It wasn't a furry black glove underneath. The fur was *Teer's*, fur attached to his body, actual fur on hands that didn't quite look human. The palm had pads, like a cat's, for chrissakes.

"Okay...okay," Bruce said softly, turning the strange hand over to check for damage. "It's one of those weird mutation things. Like that Jojo dude. No big deal. Sorry I freaked out. Though I get the gloves now."

He cleaned off both furred hands, none of the blood Teer's, and moved on to his poor, glass-cut head. As he parted it, the hair felt odd too, also more like fur, but maybe that made sense. He worked gingerly to pull out the remaining splinters and dab at the bleeding gashes, Teer leaning against him and muttering. The oddly trusting gesture made Bruce's heart ache. It wasn't as if Teer really trusted him. In his confused state, he probably thought someone familiar and loved was there taking care of him.

"Attaboy, we're almost done." Bruce kept his voice soft and gentle since it seemed to help. "I'd feel a hell of a lot better if you'd let me take you to the ER."

"No," Teer whispered, the threat of seeing a doctor apparently bringing him around. "No hospitals. Please." He gripped the lapels of Bruce's coat, then yanked his hands back, staring at them, making that strange fluttery sound.

"All right. Just don't die on me."

As soon as the words were out, Bruce's throat closed up and he gave up talking in favor of getting up to see if Teer's bed was in any shape to have him in it. He stalked to the bedroom, angry that he was upset, upset that he was angry, and stopped short in the doorway. There was no bed. Where the bed might normally have been was a board on two cinderblocks. No, it was a door. Someone's cast-off hollow-core interior door without even a pillow or a blanket to alleviate the monkish austerity.

"Well, fuck me sideways, I can't let him rest on *that*."

Shaking his head, Bruce returned to find Teer curled up on the floor, his little furred hands twitching. *So weird, but they're almost...cute, damn it.* The floor cushions would work. He pulled off Teer's boots, ones with only two-inch heels, and decided the bloodstained clothes really should go too. One hand positioned to support Teer's head, Bruce moved him carefully to lay his upper body on the largest floor cushion. It would have to do.

The orange shirt—silk, for god's sake—had fussy buttons at the throat that had Bruce cussing inventively. He took off his coat, all the effort was making him sweat despite the chill of Teer's apartment. When he got the buttons open, he found more...fur at the base of Teer's throat, then more on his chest. It wasn't just a lot of chest hair like some guys had. No, this was an actual pelt, smooth and thick like an arctic fox. When he opened the shirt further, it just got worse. Where Teer's bellybutton should have been was a slit, partially hidden by the fur, but not something an umbilical cord would've attached to. Ever.

"The fuck," Bruce whispered and jerked his hands away. He glanced up to find Teer watching him, his dark eyes finally clear and present again.

"You shouldn't have done that," Teer said, an odd note of sorrow in his voice.

"Who...what *are* you?" Bruce whispered. "You're not human."

Teer rolled onto his back, staring at the ceiling. He didn't look well, but at least he wasn't raving in another language anymore. "Bruce...the expression 'not from around here' is more applicable to me than anyone on the planet."

"You're an alien? Holy shit!" Bruce narrowed his eyes, horrible thoughts occurring suddenly. "How many more of you are there? What do you want with us?"

"There are no others," Teer whispered, the sorrow in those few words heavy enough to shatter an iron heart. "I am alone. And now you will call the authorities and I will be imprisoned."

Bruce sat back, regarding the furry alien on the floor with surprise. "You're a complete badass. You could kill me and no one would know."

"I don't wish to kill you. You are...clumsy and loud, but you have tried to be kind to me in your own way." Teer pulled in another long breath through his teeth. It seemed to be his version of a sigh. "I was exiled here, as a point too far from my home to return. There are no evil plans to invade or enslave your people."

"You're all alone? No way back?" Bruce turned that over a few times. *I should be freaked-out by this. Completely freaked-out.* The fact that he wasn't might have had more to do with how disconnected from the world he had become. Maybe it was Teer himself, soft-spoken and usually so gentle that calmed him. Maybe he just didn't care what species someone was when that person needed help. "Shit. That sucks. No rescue ship coming? Ever?"

"Never."

"So, you're like...from Alpha Centauri or something?"

"Why are you not more upset about this?" Teer ran a furry hand over his eyes.

Bruce shrugged. "Don't really know. I guess 'cause I kinda got to know you first? At least a little? I mean, if Mike had suddenly told me he was an ET or something..." He couldn't finish the thought. *Wouldn't have mattered if Mike was some hellmouth demon. Would've still loved him.*

"So you won't be calling the authorities?"

"Oh hell no. You're a complete weirdo, but you're just trying to get by like the rest of us. Feds don't have any right to haul you away and cut you up to see how you're different."

"Thank you." Teer was quiet a moment, looking at the pads on his hands. He flexed his fingers and black claws emerged. At least that explained the torn gloves. "It's a relief, in a way. That someone knows."

Bruce settled cross-legged on the carpet. Alien or not, there was still a head wound involved and he'd rather keep Teer talking for a little longer. "I get that. Hiding can't be easy. So where are you from?"

"The coordinates would be meaningless to you," Teer said on one of those sad little flutter sounds that seemed to be a sound of distress or pain. "We call the planet Irasol. I am Irasolan."

"Yeah, guess that was a stupid question," Bruce grumbled. He might as well have said he was Vulcan since the answer didn't mean a damn thing. "Were you a florist there? And why the hell exile a florist, anyway?"

Teer snorted. "No. I was not a florist. Could I

trouble you for some ice? I have bags of it in the freezer."

When Bruce walked to the freezer to check, he found a freezer packed with ice and nothing else. Out of curiosity, he opened the fridge and frowned. The empty whiteness stared back at him, broken only by a single KFC container. He wrapped some ice in a towel and went back to Teer. "You getting enough to eat?"

"Yes." Teer lowered his arm from his eyes, obviously puzzled by the question.

"There's nothing in your fridge. Or your damn freezer. You just eating fast food crap?"

Teer took the ice out of the towel and pressed it directly to his head. "That's better. Thank you. Food has been...a bit difficult. I have yet to find better sources, but I admit I haven't tried hard."

"There are supermarkets, you know." Though the minute Bruce said it, he realized that maybe Teer didn't know or didn't really understand. "Big stores full of food. Fresh, frozen, whatever you want. You can cook it yourself. Eat it raw. Hell, I don't know what works best for you."

"Depends on the meat."

Bruce squinted at him, trying to determine if Teer had any clue how suggestive that sounded. Tough to say, he spoke in such a serious deadpan all the time. "Yeah. Um. So what did you do? Before?"

"I thought by avoiding the subject it was clear I didn't wish to discuss it."

"Oh. Well, sorry. Some of us don't do subtle."

"Evidently not," Teer said in that same dry, patient tone. "I apologize for having caused you concern. But I'm feeling much more myself now."

"That's subtle-speak for 'get the hell out of my apartment,' I guess." Bruce got up, though he didn't feel good about leaving Teer alone in a nearly empty apartment. "That door, board, whatever in there. You sleep all right on that?"

"Quite comfortably. Human beds are far too soft." Teer sat up, water dripping down his arm from the melting ice. "Thank you. For coming to my rescue."

"Like you needed it."

"Perhaps not, but to have someone who wished to... Thank you."

Bruce made sure Teer could stand on his own and then let himself out of the apartment. Any minute now, he'd wake up and everything would be normal. No alien encounter, no strange conversations, and Teer would still just be the weird little man at the florist. But he wasn't waking up and he couldn't stop worrying about someone who wasn't even human.

TEER UNDRESSED SLOWLY, PUT THE TORN GLOVES ON the floor by the bed to assess later, and set his boots carefully in the closet. The night out had been his answer to Molly's constant haranguing about going out to "have fun." Bars were one of the places, apparently, to seek human fun. While some of the humans there obviously had been enjoying themselves, it had been an anxious hour for Teer.

Too many bodies in too tight a space, too many variables, and possibilities for encounters gone wrong. There would be no more of that sort of fun. Not to mention the fact that human males became even more aggressive when consuming intoxicants. He hadn't considered that until too late. It was a hard lesson to absorb, even knowing that humans often used aggression for childish reasons, for anger, for spite, for alienating otherness.

He would never make the same mistake again.

Curled up on his bed, the wood texture still odd against his fur instead of the smooth stone his body longed for, his mind replayed the evening. The first shout had startled him, but he had increased his pace and strode on. When the men surrounded him in the alley, his heart had plummeted. He feared doing damage and giving himself away. Terror of the local authorities discovering him made him slow to react.

But then Bruce had come wearing his usual angry face, anger directed at Teer's attackers. Bruce, whom he had dismissed as an ill-tempered lout, appeared worried for *him*. Suddenly, it wasn't about avoiding suspicion any longer. He had to protect Bruce, so he had acted swiftly and decisively.

Instinct, to protect. He was still Irasolan-sa even if he had lost the right to honor, *arn*, and home.

CHAPTER FIVE

A Date Is Not a Fruit

"Teer, hon, you look a little beat this morning. You okay?" Molly stopped her bustling to squint at him.

"I'm fine." Teer hesitated, drumming his gloved fingers. He knew the subject would make Molly unhappy, but he wanted her advice. "There was an altercation...a scuffle..."

"What? Someone hit you? When was this?"

"On Friday night. I went out as you said I should. But some men took a dislike to me. I'm afraid I hit some of them. Bruce said—"

"Bruce? Bruce who?"

"Mr. Bruce? He comes here every Friday for his hyacinth?"

"You went out with Bruce Bering?"

"With? Ah...no. He came across the altercation."

"Oh. I see. So he came to the rescue."

Teer shook his head, uncertain how Molly had so thoroughly derailed his narrative. "In a way. Yes. That was his intent. But Bruce said that when I struck the men, it was in self-defense and that this is allowed. Is that true?"

"How many were there?"

"Five."

"Five? Oh my god, Teer. And they cornered you? They hit you?"

"Yes."

Molly took his face between her hands. He tried not to flinch as she spoke in even, hard tones, "Now you listen to me, Teer Horath. You're a good person. You don't deserve to be treated like that. You have every right to defend yourself. Did you call the police?"

Teer twitched back from her in surprise. "Why would I do that?"

"To have them arrested. To press charges. If no one does, guys like that think they can keep gay bashing 'cause nothing ever happens."

Gay bashing. He tried the phrase out in his mind and thought he understood. "So they pursued me, wanted to hurt me, because they thought I might like to have relations with other men?"

Molly rubbed both hands over her face, a signal of frustration. "Yes. Yes! That's exactly what they were doing. Because they're douchebag idiots. And you should've called the police. *Bruce* should've called the police."

"Molly, I'm not here quite legally," Teer reminded her.

Her mouth turned down, the lines around her eyes deepening. "Damn it. I forget, sometimes. It's still not right. It's just not right."

At least he was certain of the legalities. He had

been acting in a legal fashion to defend himself and Bruce. While he couldn't make his report to the authorities regarding his attackers, at least he could be certain they wouldn't either.

"I'll stop harassing you, sorry. And I'm glad you're okay." Molly patted his gloved hand and went back to her orders.

The shop was empty, but the Christmas display tables needed filling in. Molly had predicted the special holiday plants would sell like "griddlecakes." Whatever those were, the plants had been selling quickly, and he often had to fill the empty spaces two or three times in a day. Seven poinsettias later, he began to pick out Christmas cacti to fill in, trying to keep the best possible balance of available colors since many had begun to blossom. He debated taking the last yellow one out of the stockroom. There had been fewer of the yellow and once this sold, there would be no more. Twice, he placed it on the table and took it away again. The pale yellow buds were so like an *alna* it hurt his insides to part with it.

It's not yours. It can't be, so stop being childish.

Finally, he placed it at the front of the table where everyone walking in would see it. He stroked a gloved finger gently over a thick green leaf, his vision darkening with his distress. This might be a short exile if his sanity slipped much farther. Throwing himself into researching the planet and its humans had helped him hold on, assimilation as an academic exercise, but the *strangeness* of it all was taking its toll. His skin itched under alien clothes. His desire to make normal sounds and to hear normal speech nearly choked him sometimes. The scents, the flavors, the quality of the light that sometimes made his head ache, everything hammered at his senses without respite with *nothing* familiar on which to cling.

Except this...this...which is almost familiar and still not. I will go mad soon. Then they will surely lock me away somewhere.

"Hey."

The deep voice behind him made him twitch, the fur on his arms standing on end with the shock. He whirled, eyes half-hooded, and found Bruce beside him.

"Okay there?" Bruce's frown deepened. "Didn't mean to scare you."

Teer pulled air through tightened nostrils, forcing calm on his overstimulated body. "I was thinking. You surprised me. It's not Friday."

"No, it's not." Bruce's forehead creased, then smoothed abruptly. "Oh yeah. I'm here off schedule. Just wanted to make sure you were okay."

"I'm well, thank you."

"Good. That's good." Bruce glanced around the shop as he stuffed his hands in his jacket pockets. "I, um, also came to see if I could take you to dinner after your shift is done. You know, make sure you're eating something besides crap."

Teer stared up at him, completely off balance and at a loss as to what response would be correct. "Could you excuse me? I'll...be back in just a moment."

Feeling a proper coward, Teer fled into the back room where Molly was finishing a bouquet of lilies and Shasta daisies. He stood at the end of the worktable, hands clenched together, suddenly unable to speak.

"Teer? Honey, what in the world's the matter?"

"Bruce is here," Teer blurted out.

"Okay, that's unusual, but it's no reason to get upset."

"He...he has invited me to dinner this evening."

Molly's head jerked up. Then she smiled. "Did he? That's wonderful. But why are you so nervous? Don't you want to go out with him? You don't like him? What did he say?"

Word for word, he told her, and Molly's smile widened. "It's a date, then."

"A...date? Those small dried fruits you eat sometimes?"

"No, silly. This kind of date's not a fruit. It's when two people go somewhere to enjoy each other's company."

"What's proper to say?" Teer asked her, feeling lost and foolish.

Molly set a hand on her hip. "Really? It's not that hard. If you'd like to go out with him, say 'yes, I'd love to.' And if you don't, say 'no, thank you.'"

"As simple as that? No intermediary? No references I should ask for?"

She shook her head as she turned him and gave him a gentle shove toward the front of the shop. "Go. Either yes or no. We don't do all that old-fashioned stuff here."

Teer shook his head to clear the hair from his eyes and settle the *lepi* rings in his ear, and strode back out to where Bruce stood looking flummoxed.

"Yes."

"Yes, you'll come to dinner with me?" Bruce waited until Teer nodded confirmation. Then Bruce nearly smiled. It was the beginnings of a smile, at least.

"Great. I mean, it's good. We'll get some real food in you. When are you done?"

"At six."

"I'll be back then." Bruce turned and left the shop.

At least he knows better than to expect normal human interaction. Teer sucked in a breath, wondering if he had just made a terrible mistake, and tried to put the impending invitation out of his mind.

AT FIVE MINUTES TO SIX, BRUCE PULLED INTO AN open space in front of Benson's. He debated going inside, but managed to hesitate long enough that Teer came out. Again, he had no coat, something Bruce would need to discuss with him. As the temps plummeted, that would look weirder and weirder. He did look good, though, his work apron off, wearing a cream and blue batik-design shirt with a blue scarf and blue leather pants tucked into blue suede boots with high, chunky heels and laces all the way up to his knees.

On him, it worked, the sinuous lines caressing his lean, athletic little body, his heel stalking more graceful than most women Bruce knew. Androgynous —that was the word. The set of his shoulders, the hard upper body both screamed male, but he didn't seem to have a *package*, large or small, in those tight pants. Of course, being alien, who the hell knew what being male meant for him.

Bruce got out of the car and opened the passenger door. "Hey. All set? Are you hungry?"

"Yes, I suppose I am," Teer said as he stepped into the car. "It was last Thursday, I think."

"What was last Thursday?" Bruce leaned down to peer in at him. "Holy—you haven't eaten in five days?"

Teer blinked at him and then shifted in his seat. "I don't eat every day, Bruce. I have a more efficient metabolic system out of necessity."

"Get your seat belt on," Bruce growled, needing to say something. When he got in the car, he gave Teer one more appraising look. "Not gonna fall over on me, are you? Is five days normal?"

"It is, perhaps, at the far end of normal. No, I won't faint from hunger."

"Taking your word for it," Bruce grumbled and eased off the curb for the drive downtown to Fifth Avenue.

"You look nice this evening," Teer said in that same calm tone he used for just about every damn thing.

"Thanks. Molly tell you to say that?"

"No." Teer dropped his gaze to his hands, the work gloves replaced by blue leather. "Yes. But the red is a good, strong color for you. I do like it."

It didn't make a lot of sense, but a warm pocket settled in Bruce's chest at the compliment. He'd picked out the shirt with Teer's tastes in mind, after all. But since when did he pick out shirts with anything in mind? Other than how clean it was?

During the drive, he interrogated Teer about his diet, what things he actually could eat. Vegetables and fruits were hit or miss, but didn't seem to bother him in small quantities. Same thing with grains, so the flour coating on his fried chicken only caused a little discomfort. Potatoes, strangely enough, didn't work at all. Poor little guy had tried some fries and ended up with crippling stomach cramps.

"Fish?"

Teer shook his head. "I don't know. We have no sea creatures at home. We have no sea. So I have been reluctant to try."

"Cheese? Any dairy-type stuff?"

"I have developed a...fondness for milk." Teer's tongue ran over his bottom lip before he seemed to catch himself. "Again, large quantities are difficult."

"And how would you know that?"

Again, Teer shifted, tucking his hands under his thighs and then clutching them together in his lap. "I drank an entire container once. The taste was intoxicating."

"Oh hell. That'd be bad for even human stomachs." Bruce tucked the information away, though. For someone who ate maybe twice a week, binging on something sounded off. So milk triggered a weird response, like some people had to chocolate or alcohol.

Bruce had chosen a local brewpub as somewhere casual but not dive-y, one where the food was top-notch and the place only got loud on the weekends. He had reservations and escorted Teer to the booth by the window since he figured his companion wasn't comfortable sitting with his back to half a room of people. With the grilled salmon for him and steak for Teer, he ordered a beer flight as well so Teer could try some.

"Well?"

Teer put the last of the glasses down, the stout. He

had taken a tiny, careful sip of each. "Beer is dreadful. You enjoy this?"

"Hell, yeah."

"It is an intoxicant?"

"For us. Don't know if it would be for you."

Teer nodded. "I think it would be. But the taste is like drinking bitter bread. Are there milk intoxicants?"

"There are drinks with milk in them. Don't want you getting falling down drunk, though," Bruce said with a frown. "Maybe we'll try one when you're at home, okay? Just so you're not out in public if it ends up being a bad idea."

"Ah. Yes." Teer stared around the restaurant at the waitstaff, at other patrons, at the wood-beamed ceiling, clearly uncomfortable.

"So. How long have you been here?" Bruce brought his attention back to the table.

"Several months."

"And Molly gave you a job without a social or a license or anything?"

"She needed help and perhaps felt pity for me. She pays me 'under the table,' she says, which I assume means out of sight of the authorities." Teer tipped his head to the side. "Interrogation is part of being on a date?"

"Not interrogation." Bruce frowned. *Is that what I was doing?* "But time to get to know each other. Questions are normal for that."

"So I may interro—ask you questions?"

Bruce shrugged. "Sure. If I don't want to answer, I won't. Same goes for you."

"Agreed." Teer pushed his water glass around,

watching the ice cubes. "What do you do? Your occupation?"

"Easy one. I'm a pilot. Qualified to fly most small craft, but right now I fly seaplanes. Take tourists and hunters in and out of the wilderness. Sometimes researchers."

"And do you work under the table?"

"Oh hell no. That'd be tougher for a pilot. Have to be licensed. I work for a charter company. Trying to go it on my own got too dicey."

Teer nodded, still staring at the water. "I will ask something now that you may not wish to answer. The hyacinth every Friday, who is it for?"

None of your damn business... The snarl was almost out, but damn it, he knew Teer's secret, the one that left him isolated and constantly on edge. It was only fair. "They're for Mike's grave. My lover...my partner. Probably would've been my husband if this damn state allowed it."

A gloved hand crept over to cover his. "Your *arn*, your life partner. I am sorry. This is why you are always so angry."

"I am?" *Yeah, I am.* "Guess so."

"Would it be too much of an intrusion to ask how he died?"

Bruce downed one of the beer samples, barely tasting it, and knocked back a second. *Waste of good beer, you idiot.* "Mike was a pilot too. It was an accident. A crash. Medical call in bad weather. He thought he could make it. The floats caught on landing. Plane flipped. Died in the water."

"So much water," Teer murmured. "Your heart lies broken in that water."

"Yeah. Not much I can do about it." Bruce turned his palm up and gave the smaller hand in his a little squeeze, blinking back the sting in his eyes. "What about you? Now that I spilled my guts. Are you a criminal or something that they exiled you?"

Teer snatched his hand back, a brief spark in his eyes that quickly died. "No. I am no lawbreaker."

"Good to know. But I bet they don't exile people to the ass end of space with us barbarians for mistakes on their tax forms."

"I suppose that was a joke," Teer said distantly. He pressed the back of one gloved hand to his eye socket as if willing away a headache. "It was a broken oath, a complete stripping of honor that brought me here. No. I won't tell the story. I will tell you I was commander of... No, that's not important, either. But I was born *sa*. A class, caste perhaps, of Irasolan sworn to protect. I failed."

Bruce tried to follow at least the gist of what Teer was saying. "You were born military? So you, what, trained from when you were a kid?"

"Yes." Teer licked the condensation off the side of his glass but didn't drink. "Those men who attacked me...so many unfair advantages. I am trained. Efficient in the use of necessary force. Your gravity is somewhat less than my home."

"And they were really stupid."

"There is that."

Bruce patted Teer's arm. "Sorry. That got all kinds of heavy. No more talking about our sorry pasts. What do you do when you're not at the shop?"

"I am in my...at my apartment."

"Okay, great. But you don't just stare at the walls,

do you?" *Those sad, empty walls. Hell, maybe he likes it that way.*

"No. I research things that puzzle me and watch the television."

Bruce gave him a sideways glance as the food arrived. He waited until the staff cleared out and Teer had a chance to try his steak. A couple of people at nearby tables stared at the spectacle of a man in pretty gloves eating with the dainty manners of some eighteenth-century dandy. Bruce glared at the curious diners, who hastily looked away.

"You do know that most of the stuff on TV's pretend, right?"

Teer swallowed a tiny bite of steak. "I'm foreign, Bruce, not a child. I know the difference between informative programming and entertainment. But I watch movies and fictional shows to understand human attitudes better. What you find important. What you find distasteful or humorous."

"Oh. I guess that's good. Even though a lot of TV shows are really stupid. I hope they're not giving you the wrong idea."

"Things puzzle me." Teer carefully moved his steak away from the mashed potatoes. "This is wonderful. I think I like steak. Humor is the most difficult for me. But I find in some ways we are similar. Humans value family, though the definition is fluid. Humans honor a sense of duty and displays of courage, though they do not all aspire to these things."

"Guess we are kinda confusing." Bruce attacked his salmon, beautifully cooked with a lemon-garlic sauce. "Humans don't always understand humans."

"I am trying," Teer said, an edge to his soft voice.

He put his utensils down and squeezed his eyes shut with his palms flat on the table. "Perhaps it is a foolish struggle."

"Hey..." Bruce reached over to take his hand again, since he seemed okay with that. "Hey. You're doing great. Amazing, really. Damn it. I keep upsetting you."

"There's so much water. So much...of everything. I feel sometimes as if I were suffocating under a rockslide. Simply too much."

The booth should have been one of those semicircular ones instead of two facing benches. Then he could've pulled Teer over and hugged him tight. But he didn't know if that would help or make things worse. Maybe Irasolans didn't do the physical comfort thing.

"Teer, look at me." Bruce squeezed the hand he held. "You need to go home?"

"Home," Teer whispered, the heartbreak contained in that single word making Bruce regret he'd said it. Then Teer shook his head and sat up straighter. "No, thank you. I'm sorry. I'm making this unpleasant for you and you were so kind to invite me."

"Nah. Don't worry about it." Bruce sat back again to give Teer room to breathe. It had to be hard, everything so strange and no one to talk to. "Eat your damn steak. That's why we're here."

Teer offered a half smile. "I can't possibly eat all of this. Even half will make me ill. How do humans consume so much? Or when they can't, why do they waste so much?"

"Different biology," Bruce grunted as he plowed through his salmon. With a few quick scoops, he transferred the mashed potatoes to his plate and gave

Teer two of his asparagus spears. "Try those. See if you like them. Anyway, some humans eat way more than they should. Not healthy. I'm a big guy. I need a lot of food. Why people waste so much, I can't answer. Not everyone does, but it's a bad habit. People not thinking."

"But they will throw this in the refuse bin if I am unable to finish?"

"Hell, no. We're gonna have them put it in a nice container and you take that home with you. Put it in the fridge for later."

For the first time that evening, Teer's eyes brightened. "Oh! What a lovely thought. What do they call this practice?"

"Used to call it a doggy bag. For you, we'll just call it leftovers."

"Good. Leftovers." Teer took a tiny bite of asparagus, swallowed it with obvious difficulty, then went back to his tiny bites of steak with pleased little sounds that sent shivers up Bruce's back.

No. Just no. I can't be thinking things like that. He's an alien, for fuck's sake.

Teer licked his bottom lip and the shiver returned. Yes, alien, but he was heartbreakingly beautiful in his own way, vulnerable and desperately lonely. Bruce wanted to wrap him up tight, wanted to make the pain go away, and he had no idea where the urge came from.

Just so he could hear more of those soft, pleased growls, Bruce ordered a slice of cheesecake for them to share for dessert.

CHAPTER SIX

Delayed Transition Shock

Despite Bruce's insistence on asking indelicate questions, Teer found he had enjoyed the evening. With his cardboard box from the restaurant in his lap and a belly uncomfortably full of meat and, oh mother of seeds, *cheesecake*, he drowsed in the passenger seat on the drive home.

Bruce pulled onto the now-familiar street and parked beside Teer's apartment building. "Want me to come up for a bit?"

"Come up?"

"Yeah, it's early. I could keep you company. Kinda nice to watch a movie with someone else sometimes."

That did sound attractive. He had never been one of those who needed constant companionship as some males did. Teer's last second-in-command had been a company-needy sort, always after him to join this group or that. But while Teer enjoyed his time alone, he had never spent *all* of his off-duty time alone. The isolation wore on his nerves.

"Yes. Please come up."

In the apartment, Bruce settled awkwardly on one of the floor cushions without complaint and helped Teer choose a movie to watch. They agreed on *Master and Commander* since Bruce thought highly of it and Teer was fascinated by the vessels used to navigate the planet's enormous bodies of water prior to the development of propulsion engines. He found himself edging closer to Bruce's warmth during horrifying scenes where the waves grew violent and men died, not in battle but because of the terrible ferocity of the water.

"They are playacting. They have not drowned," he whispered, and Bruce slid an arm around him.

"It's all pretend," Bruce murmured close to his ear. "You need to stop the movie?"

"No... I... It's simply difficult for me to grasp. How deep is this ocean?"

Bruce tugged him closer so Teer rested against his chest. "Well, around the Galapagos, it's about a thousand feet deep, I think. Probably close to nine thousand in the deeper parts."

Nine thousand feet? Nine thousand? Teer's ceilings in his apartment were eight feet high. He had measured to gain some sense of the local unit of length. So the building in which he lived was no more than fifty feet high. More than one hundred and eighty of his apartment buildings deep? He wrapped an arm around Bruce's sturdy chest and clung there, dizzy and nauseous. "Oh."

"Sorry." Bruce rubbed his back gently. "I'm thinking you didn't need to know that. Not a lot of deep water where you're from, huh?"

Teer nestled closer against Bruce's side. It felt so

good to have real physical contact again. Often considered odd and solitary among his own people, even he hadn't been in the habit of sleeping alone. Onboard ship, officers shared beds, sleeping in tangled heaps. The strange human habit of each in his own bed was one of the most shocking for him.

"Irasol is more like the deserts here. There is water, but much is ice or underground. Where there are streams and pools in the caves, none are deep enough that you would sink."

"But you have plants?"

"Precious, carefully husbanded, yes. Cultivated by the *re*, those of my race born to tend the plants."

"You really don't have any choice, do you? You're born military, so that's what you do. Or plant-tender, and that's what you do. What if you'd wanted to be something else?"

Teer lifted his head to stare at Bruce. "Why would I? We are born where we need to be. Our bloodlines are uniquely suited to each *menan*, each class."

"But you got kicked out. So you couldn't have been that good at it."

Anger scratched at the back of Teer's mind. He carefully packed it away. Bruce had no way to understand, no familiar comparison. "I was good. I was very good. General is the closest translation I can find here for my rank. Being suited to something doesn't guarantee success. I was one of the best and still failed."

"Yeah," Bruce agreed softly. "You're right there."

They were quiet for a long while, each struggling in his own memories, holding tight to keep those storms at bay. When one of the officers in the movie shot the doctor, in what Teer felt was an act of incredible incompetence, he began to ask questions again, about the old projectile weapons and about the Galapagos, which Bruce answered as best he could. Teer had to give him credit. When he didn't know something, he said so. One could become attached to such honesty.

The movie ended, signaled by the words that rolled across the screen, always too fast for Teer to read properly. Bruce came to his rescue there, as well, explaining that these were the "credits," the listing of everyone involved. It was an impressive list. Storytelling was quite an undertaking for humans. They took it quite seriously, marshaling as many people as some species would need for battle.

With the ending music still playing, Teer took off his gloves and let his bare hand rest on Bruce's shirt. It was a heavy material, but soft. He wasn't certain what it was called. So much that was considered masculine here was heavy, dark, cumbersome, but sometimes the heaviness was countered with something more elegant, more graceful.

If he closed his eyes, if he ignored the scent, he could pretend he rested in Irasolan arms. *For just a moment. Let me have but a moment.* Bruce took his hand, shattering the illusion, his broad thumb stroking Teer's pads.

"Bruce," Teer whispered, trying to stifle little pleasured purrs. "Those are sensitive."

"Hmm."

The sound was so close to a pleased Irasolan growl, Teer's cock threatened to descend. Bruce tugged the scarf from around Teer's neck, caressing the fur at the base of his throat.

"Your fur's so soft. Crap. Do you even call it fur?"

Teer drew in a careful breath. Where was this going? Bruce couldn't possibly have any *desire* for him. The lack of desire was mutual...wasn't it? "It's... Since you have no word for it, fur. Yes."

Maybe it wasn't desire, but there was obviously a shared curiosity. Teer slid his hand up Bruce's chest and undid the first button. When the only reaction that elicited was Bruce's hand mimicking his, Teer continued, baring Bruce's broad chest. Irreverent and misplaced joy pierced him at the sight of that furred expanse. The human males on the television were always hairless. Bruce, oh stars...Bruce had a *pelt*.

He nuzzled at the fur, more coarse and wiry than Irasolan chest pelts, but the texture wasn't unpleasant. Bruce's breath caught when he nudged against one of the two nubs at about midchest. Nipples. He knew what they were for in human females, but had yet to understand why males had them as well. Perhaps they were purely pleasure nerve-bundles.

Bruce's hand slid down his chest. Sometime in the past few seconds, Teer's shirt had been unbuttoned as well. Without palm pads, it felt strange, rough in the fingertips but too smooth in the palm as Bruce petted and stroked Teer's chest pelt. He stilled when Bruce's fingers brushed his *lunamon*. The entrance to his brood pouch was far too intimate for mere curiosity. Teer shivered and curled in on himself, lightning jolts of pleasure pressing his cock down from its resting place inside his crotch.

"What's this?" Bruce murmured, fingers brushing over the slit again. "It's not like a bellybutton. And it sure as hell seems to get you going."

Teer couldn't help the rumbling purr that escaped. He hadn't been touched in so long. "It's...oh please... it's where the ovipositor would go. If you were female. Where the fertile eggs would..."

He gasped when Bruce slid a finger inside, gentle, tentative, but still too much. "Great mother of seeds!" he called out in his own language, squirming against the touch he wasn't certain he wanted and the tight confines of pants not meant to accommodate a descending erection. The *lunamon* tightened and clenched even as he ejaculated, the double orgasm painful in its intensity, completely mortifying in its suddenness. He wrenched away from Bruce, panting, and scrambled to his feet, pulse pounding in distress.

"I think you should go," he whispered, blunt and rude in his overwhelming confusion, turning away to hide the spreading wetness at the front of his pants.

"I'm so damn sorry." Bruce got up as well, one hand held out toward him. "I went too far. Should've asked—"

"Go. Please, go."

"Teer?"

"Now."

With his back turned, he couldn't see Bruce's expression, afraid of what he might see, but the door clicked shut a moment later. Distress and shame warred with anger, the floor tilting dizzily beneath his feet under the onslaught of confusion.

None of my lovers have ever done that for me, brought on the double climax so swiftly. And now this human, with hardly a touch...

Teer's claws extended. With an anguished howl, he ripped the human clothes from his body, shredding them into rags on the carpet. Everything was wrong, *everything*. The sounds, the scents, the taste of food, the quality of the light, the ground under his feet, the very *air* around him, all wrong! He hated this place, hated the wrongness, the constant itch under his skin and in his brain.

The maelstrom of confused rage consumed him. All thought whited out in the storm, Teer fled into the dark, heading north into the wilds.

CHAPTER SEVEN

World's Smallest Bigfoot

"How much are these?" Bruce pointed to the display of Christmas cacti, the ones Teer had been admiring longingly the day before. Maybe a combination apology and early Christmas present would help repair the damage.

"Why?" Molly glared at him, the question unexpected from a storeowner.

"I thought...Teer might like one? Maybe two?"

"What the hell happened yesterday, Bering? What did you do?"

Bruce grimaced. "He's still upset, huh?"

"I wouldn't know. He didn't show up for work and he's not answering his phone." Molly pointed an accusing finger at him. "All I know is Teer's the most reliable employee I've ever had and then he goes out with you and *poof*! Vanishes."

"Damn it. I knew he was mad at me..." Bruce trailed off to return the glare. "Look, I didn't hurt him. Didn't do anything awful. It was a culture clash thing. Anyone been to his place to check on him?"

Molly's shoulders slumped, her aggressive stance melting into worry. "No. It's not like I can leave the shop without anyone else here."

"Yeah. Sorry." *Not really my fault he freaked out. Is it? I don't even know what the hell happened.* "I'll go check on him. Even if he won't talk to me, at least we'll know he's okay."

Bruce picked out two plants hoping Teer would accept a peace offering, the yellow one that had captivated Teer and a salmon-colored one, and asked Molly to hold them for him. The drive over to Teer's building flashed by in a haze of worry, terrible scenarios playing out in his mind. He'd known an exchange student in college who had attempted suicide because of culture-shock depression. *Please don't be stupid, Teer. Don't do anything just because you feel bad now.*

Weirdest thing was, Bruce didn't have a clue why he cared so much. Sure, he'd felt bad at first for snarling at someone whose only crime was being different. Then he'd gotten all protective and shit over someone who was horribly alone. But that wasn't all of it. Teer was a badass who didn't need him. He was a military man with a past, obviously educated and intelligent, a quick thinker and a survivor, all things that pushed Bruce's buttons hard.

He's not even a man, though. He's a freaking alien. With fur. And claws. He couldn't even figure out whether he should be ashamed or not for being turned on by Teer's nuzzling. It was sort of like bestiality, wasn't it? *Fuck, it's confusing.*

A spot was open in front of Teer's building. Bruce did a half-assed parking job and raced up the steps two at a time. At Teer's door, he knocked softly and then louder when he didn't hear anything.

"Teer? You in there?" Bruce hoped all of his neighbors were at work, but if they got mad, fuck 'em. "Come on, General! I know you're pissed at me, but Molly's worried."

He tried the knob, raising an eyebrow when the door opened. "Too much of a badass to lock your door? Hey—"

The words stuck in his throat when he caught sight of the living room. While not trashed, since there was hardly anything in the living room, a pile of shredded cloth lay in a heap near the living room table, blue, cream, and purple. Bruce knelt next to the pile, fingering the torn pieces. *His shirt and pants, one of the pillows...fuck. Even what's left of his blue boots.*

"Teer?" Bruce stomped through the apartment, checking every possible hiding place, even under the door bed. There was no sign of Teer. His toothbrush was dry. The light blinking on his landline showed unchecked messages.

Heartsick and anxious, Bruce fished a crumpled receipt out of his coat pocket and left a note.

Hey. Stopped by to check if you're okay. We're worried. At least give Molly a call if you can't talk to me.
  -Bruce

He walked the neighborhood the rest of that afternoon, popping into stores and bars just in case Teer had needed a change of scenery. After dark, he gave up and went home to his house in Rogers Park. Why he hadn't sold the damn thing, he couldn't say. A four-bedroom two-story was too big for one person, but it had seemed the perfect size when Mike was there. Mike took up a lot of space, physically, psychically, possession-wise. He had meant to start giving away some of Mike's things too, the things Mike's mother hadn't claimed on her one visit after his death.

Every time Bruce packed something up to give away—Mike's clothes, his tree carvings, even his magazines—he ended up unpacking them again. They were going to have dogs someday, maybe even kids...

Bruce opened the door with an angry shove. *Damn Teer for leaving...*

Wait. That should have been Mike, not Teer. Where had that come from? He hung his coat on the rack, shucked his boots by the door, and went to the kitchen to heat up some uninspired box from the freezer for another lonely dinner in front of the TV.

THE SNOW TASTED ODD, A LITTLE METALLIC, BUT better than the water in his apartment. His previous apartment, Teer supposed. Going back now would do no good. The flight from the city, from shadow to shadow, had been harrowing. Without human clothes, he couldn't risk a return journey. Not to mention, Molly would believe him unreliable by now and would never take him back. Without employment, he would soon lose the rented space in his building.

He had acted stupidly in a moment of confusion

and despair. Now he would pay for it with a severely shortened lifespan. He could survive comfortably if the weather continued as it had, but he understood that the temperature would plummet over the next month and howling snowstorms would tax even his cold-adapted system. Alone in the cold, he would die before winter's end. Perhaps that was fitting.

Uncurling inside his den of evergreen branches, he squinted against the sunlight, too bright against the snow. Ridiculous yellow sun. Ridiculous too-bright world. He readjusted the blue scarf, a barely adequate *kurya*, around his face since he had finished drinking snow. Soon food would become an issue. The small creatures, squirrels, mice, and rabbits, were all quick and agile, difficult to catch. The larger ones like the moose and bears were far more meat than he needed and difficult to kill on his own, at any rate. Tempting, to raid traps set by human hunters, but even in his current state, he wouldn't stoop to theft.

The hunters the previous day had been a shock. At any other time, more aware of his surroundings and not as self-absorbed, he would have detected their presence long before they had stumbled on him gathering pine boughs. All of them had been equally shocked, but Teer recovered first, dropping his branches and racing off into the woods. The one hunter had shrieked. The other had taken a shot. Not a very good shot, unless it was meant to graze his shoulder. The wound ached abominably, but he had no medical supplies to ease the healing.

He would be more careful from now on, stay still, and listen often as the rabbits did. No human would surprise him again. Though the surprise with Bruce had been far more pleasant than the one with the hunters, in retrospect. If he hadn't overreacted so badly, perhaps... but no, it didn't bear considering. Bruce was still grieving his lost love, his heart still an open wound, not a good time to consider relations again no matter what species. What had happened, or nearly happened between them was best forgotten.

These strange, silent giants, the trees, would be his companions, forbidding, impossible sentinels who would bear sole witness to the final demise of General Teer.

"I SWEAR IT'S TRUE!" THE FIRST HUNTER WAS STILL yelling into his headset as they took off. "Every word of it. We couldn't make this shit up."

"You sure you boys weren't drinking some grain alcohol up here?" Bruce asked in a dry tone as he kept an eye on the approaching treetops. "Bigfoot?"

"Yeah, but he was, I dunno..." The second, calmer hunter scratched his head. "A baby Bigfoot or something. World's smallest Bigfoot. Might've been a girl Bigfoot. Had a blue scarf wrapped around its head. Wasn't any bigger than my ten-year-old. Covered in black fur. Always thought they were supposed to be brown."

Bruce's heart stuttered and he nearly banked the plane at a bad moment. "Black fur? You're sure?"

"Yeah. Sun was pretty bright. It was black fur. Took a shot at it."

"You *shot* at him?" Bruce repeated, trying to pull

breath into lungs that felt like lumpy potato sacks. *Fuck, they shot Teer. Holy—*

"Missed, though. Kept on running like its ass was on fire."

Suddenly, he could breathe again, but the constriction around his heart remained. *Concentrate, damn it.* He had to get these chuckleheads back to the seaplane base so he could come back and find Teer. No, there wasn't enough light left. He had to think up some valid reason to take the day off tomorrow and come back. *Don't run far, Teer, please.*

"Yep. World's smallest Bigfoot," the more excitable hunter said, his head bobbing up and down like he had a loose spring. "That's what it was all right."

Thank God for small favors. No one would believe these jokers, and they had no idea what they had really seen. For tonight, he had to assume Teer was safe.

Please be safe. I'm coming to find you tomorrow. I don't fucking care if I don't understand what happened between us —don't shove me away again.

SNOW HAD FALLEN THE PREVIOUS EVENING, THICK and heavy, a new experience for Teer since the snowfall on his planet had been infrequent and rarely more than a dusting. He thought at first when he woke that it was still night, but gradually his muddled brain realized that the entrance to his den was blocked. While easy to dig into, the barrier of white gave no indication of how far he would need to dig. After two hand-lengths, panic began to seep into his movements. What if there was no end and he suffocated under the snow? What if he needed to dig in a different direction, always near escape but never managing it?

Soon, the snow became brighter. His hand broke through into unobstructed air. He rested his head on his arm, relieved and chagrined over his panic. A bit of shoving with his shoulders brought him into the open, leaving a neat tunnel behind to his den. A small plane flew overhead, obscured by the branches, but it made him think of Bruce. Again.

Dozens of humans most likely flew identical small craft overhead each day. The probability of this one being Bruce was absurdly small. It didn't matter in the least. Teer had no doubt irretrievably offended him by ordering him out so abruptly after their intimate moment. He most likely had drawn the conclusion that Teer found him unattractive or perhaps that Bruce's own actions had been distasteful.

Neither one was true, but he'd been unable to communicate that at the time. While Bruce's anatomy was unfamiliar, he'd found the golden pelt unusual and appealing. The sharp, sudden onslaught of orgasm had been shocking, but not because of Bruce's actions, which had been gentle and considerate. Still, even a comforting relationship with a human was most likely dangerous. He was a fool to even dream of such things, especially now that he'd alienated the only male who would most likely ever be interested.

The drone of the plane's engine had stopped. Either the small craft had landed on the nearby lake or it had flown out of earshot. Teer shook free of the snow and, wincing a bit from the projectile graze on his shoulder, hauled himself up into the branches of the nearest tree where he had hidden a small, fat bird the day before. It wasn't quite frozen solid, his sharp back teeth managing to tear into the hardened flesh. He heaved a sigh. *Nothing like steak, but it will sustain me several days.*

Snow from the tree branch served to clean off his hands before he leaped down again, sinking nearly up to his knees in the deep snow that had drifted under his tree. He froze when an out of place sound reached his ears. A human voice called out nearby. Teer cocked his head to listen. *No. It can't be.*

The voice was faint but familiar. "Teer! Hey, Teer! Damn it, if you're here, say something!"

He shrank against the tree trunk, trying to determine the direction of the voice. It had to be Bruce. Who else would call for him out here? But he was torn as to whether he should go to him or hide from him.

"Teer! General Teer! I just want t—"

A sharp crack preceded the sudden end to Bruce's words. The choice became no choice. With a frustrated cry, Teer surged forward toward the spot Bruce's voice had been. There was only silence now. What had the sharp sound been? Gunshot? Ice breaking? With a hundred terrible things leaping up in his mind, Teer reached a spot of shallower snow and ran, the pads on his feet giving him enough traction to speed along where a human would have floundered.

"Bruce?" he called as he neared the spot. "Bruce, are you here?"

Not a shot or ice cracking—the terrible snap had been a branch breaking under the weight of snow, large enough to block his path. He stopped in horror when he spotted the gloved hand protruding partway through the long needles.

"No, you can't. You mustn't," Teer whispered as he sized up the branch for the best fulcrum point to move it. About a third of the way down from the thickest point, he shoved his shoulder underneath and heaved, toppling the branch over. Bruce lay facedown in the snow, an unnatural bend in his right forearm.

Teer dropped to his knees. Gently, cradling the broken arm, he turned Bruce onto his back, desperate for confirmation that he still breathed. "Bruce? Do you hear me?"

Human eyelids flickered open to reveal those stunning green eyes. "What the fuck?"

Belatedly, Teer recalled his modified *kurya* and clawed it from his head. "It's me. Please lie still a moment. I'm not certain how badly you're injured."

"Teer. Damn it." Bruce ignored him and sat up, all the color draining from his face as he jarred his arm. "Aw, crap."

"Why are you here?" Teer hurried to secure the broken limb, binding it to Bruce's chest with the scarf.

"I came looking for you, genius," Bruce answered, his voice uncertain and full of pain. "Fuck that hurts. I freaked you out somehow and then you were gone. Molly was worried. I was worried."

Teer put an arm around him when he swayed. "How did you find me?"

"Couple hunters I picked up saw you. They thought you were a Bigfoot. A little Bigfoot. I figured you might still be in the same area. They said they shot at you."

"Ah. They only grazed me." The hunters. Of

course. "What am I to do with you now? I have no medical equipment here."

"Come back with me. Please." Bruce gripped his hand, his eyes searching Teer's face. "You're gonna die out here. It's my fault you're out here. Please come with me."

Teer shook his head, his *lepi* rings jingling. "How am I to get you back to the city? You have only one arm to operate your vehicle."

Bruce snorted. "I can fly the damn thing with one arm."

"You brave, ridiculous thing." Teer sighed and rested his head on top of Bruce's. He closed his eyes, willing his aching brain to think. "I was atmospheric craft qualified back home. The principles must be similar."

"There, see? We've got three arms between us, not one." Bruce shuddered, in obvious pain. "So you're still pissed at me."

"I was never angry with you." Teer tightened his grip. "Can you stand? Shall I carry you?"

"There's no way a little twerp like you could carry me," Bruce said on a weary snort. "And if you weren't mad at me, why'd you kick me out the other night? Why the vanishing act?"

Teer slid an arm under Bruce's knees and lifted him, ignoring his dismayed cursing. "It was... I was overwhelmed. By everything."

Bruce slid his whole arm around Teer's shoulders to take some of his weight. "I get the culture-shock thing. That's gotta be tough. I mean, everything's probably different. Even the stars. But you were doing so good. Why right then? Why run instead of letting me help you?"

"There are—" Teer cut off when he realized he was walking aimlessly. "Which way?"

"Keep heading this way. Toward the lake."

"Ah." Of course. The plane would need clear space to land. "There are biological differences between us."

"No shit."

"I state the obvious as an introduction." Teer pulled in a slow breath, steeling himself. "Irasolan males share some reproductive traits with human males, but not others. We have male gamete production and organs similar to your penis and testicles, though they are tucked away and more sensibly protected except during mating."

"Yeah, sometimes wish mine were."

"Sensible, but biologically impractical for you." Teer steered around a huge tree, the frozen lake now in sight. It felt good to talk to someone again, even if the someone was a human. The week of isolation had been too much like the exile pod before and after jump sleep. "But we have an additional function. Once the eggs are fertilized, the female inserts her ovipositor into our *lunamon*...our brood pouch, I think you would say. We carry the young until they hatch, not the females."

"Oh." Bruce puzzled over that, then apparently made the connections. "Oh! Like seahorses. How cool is that? You get to have the babies."

"Yes." With a mental jolt, Teer realized he hadn't simply suffered from the isolation. He had missed talking to *Bruce*.

"And the thing...the slit, the opening on your

stomach, that's where the ovipositor hooks up?"

Teer nodded. "So while you have one sort of climax during intimate relations, we have a possibility for two."

He had walked several steps in silence when Bruce let out a miserable groan. Teer glanced down at him in alarm.

"Did I step wrong and jolt you? Are you going to be ill?"

"No, no... Oh God, Teer. I'm sorry. I touched stuff without asking and your body reacted and that's why you freaked out."

The plane sat to the left. Teer corrected course, keeping his steps even but trying to hurry. "You are not at fault. I want that clear." He heaved another calming breath through clenched nostrils. "You were kind and gentle. I could have stopped your hands at any time. Perhaps it was inevitable, some sort of transitional shock. But I think I may have been building up to it for some time. The, ah, unexpected climaxes simply triggered the mental break."

Bruce made an odd sound. "Climaxes? As in more than one? I did that?"

"Yes. Perhaps we could discuss the mechanics of that another time." Teer stepped carefully onto the snow-covered lake and headed for the seaplane. "When I'm somewhat more comfortable."

"Sorry. Got it." Bruce slid his arm off Teer's shoulders. "Put me down, all right? I've gotta get the doors open."

"Can you climb in on your own?"

"Don't go far. I might need some help."

With a bit of swearing and lifting, they managed to

manhandle Bruce into the pilot's seat. Teer climbed in the other side and settled, helping Bruce with his shoulder harness before fastening his own. The controls were unfamiliar, but Teer pushed, turned, and pulled as Bruce instructed, and between them, they started the engine. The basics of thrust and lift still applied, as it did in any planetary atmosphere. Following Bruce's instructions, Teer helped control the speed while Bruce handled the yoke.

They lurched a bit on takeoff, but wobbled into the air without mishap.

"Bruce."

"Yeah?"

"You look terrible."

"Thanks." Bruce settled back with a snort. "It's not far. I'll make it."

Still, Teer worried. He filled the anxious minutes with questions about the controls and the tracking systems. Good. If they crashed, at least someone would find them. He eyed the double yoke dubiously, but was glad of it when the seaplane base came into sight below them. Bruce was as pale as the clouds overhead, his voice weakening as he continued to give instructions.

Teer steadied his side of the double yoke when Bruce's arm began to shake, keeping them level and their descent steady coming in to the base. The *feel* of the plane wasn't so much different from an Irasolan single transport craft. Bruce switched to handling the speed and direction while Teer followed his instructions and kept the nose from slamming into the ice.

Together, they nosed the seaplane into its berth,

cell, whatever it was called here. By the time Bruce turned off the engines, he was shuddering violently. Teer pulled on the heavy, drab clothes Bruce had brought for him. The checked shirt and the rough blue pants were too large, but they would have to do, and Bruce had been thorough. There were boots, gloves, and even a scarf to cover the fur at the base of his throat.

"Stay here." He patted Bruce's shoulder. "Please don't move. I'll fetch assistance and have them call for medical transport."

Bruce only nodded woozily, which worried Teer even more. He hurried inside the building directly beside their landing spot and swiftly concocted an explanation involving falling into icy water and Bruce coming to his rescue. He kept the part with the tree branch, since that was true. After several interminable questions, the young female behind the desk shouted at several males nearby. They hurried out to help Bruce while the female called for medical assistance.

Soon the transport arrived, Bruce was loaded onto a stretcher, and Teer was left standing by the building, shivering with reaction. He had returned, after all. Despite his determination to die in the wilderness, here he was again, among humans. It was one thing to contemplate his own death, but he couldn't have allowed Bruce's. He wasn't certain he could bear to examine that too closely.

"Hey!" One of the medical attendants waved him over. "The big jerk won't let us load him unless you come too. Wanna ride along?"

No, no, no, I don't want to be anywhere near a human hospital. "All right." His brain had obviously become disconnected from his mouth. With a feeling of all his neural pathways severing, he climbed into the back of the vehicle, sat where they told him to, and held Bruce's hand when he seemed to need it.

"You the boyfriend?" one of the attendants asked.

Unsure where the question was leading, Teer answered cautiously, "We have dated. He is my friend."

Oddly, this seemed to satisfy him. Teer made note of that since it had turned out to be a proper and acceptable response. *And he is my friend. He came to find me.* Guilt accompanied that thought, of course, since Bruce had been injured because of him.

From there, the afternoon descended into a surreal round of staying by Bruce and being separated from him, waiting beside him and waiting for him to return. It seemed an eternity later that Teer could finally help him dress again, his broken arm stabilized and his head filled with instructions. It all seemed quite primitive. No bone regeneration. No proper pain-cessation techniques. The emergency medicine staff seemed only able to confirm that, yes, the arm was broken, which was rather obvious, and to immobilize it until Bruce could see a proper doctor. All rather inefficient.

As they settled into the back of a taxi, Bruce rested his head on the back of the seat, not quite as white but hardly able to keep his eyes open. "Give you a choice. I'll give you cab fare to your apartment or you can come with me. I've got room."

Teer weighed the two options for all of twenty seconds. "I'll come with you. You shouldn't be alone in your current condition."

And neither should I.

CHAPTER EIGHT

Human Traditions

It was weird having someone in the house again. At first, Bruce worried about thinking it was Mike. But Teer's footsteps, his movements, and his presence were so different from Mike's, Bruce never mistook him for anyone else, even early in the morning when he was groggy and half-awake.

He'd coached Teer through calling Molly, suggesting phrases like "transitional depression" and "mental breakdown" to explain his absence and his failure to call. Molly, bless her, was such a kind soul that of course she understood and took Teer back. She hadn't been able to find anyone to replace him anyway and was frantic to have him back as orders piled up closer to Christmas. New bus route mapped out, clothes retrieved from his apartment, Teer went back to work two days after returning from the wild.

Bruce felt a little guilty, but he called the shop at ten after nine. Teer had been steady and solicitous the past couple of days, but he couldn't help worrying.

"Did he get there?" he growled into the phone when Molly picked up.

"Did who...Bruce?" Molly sounded exasperated.

"Yeah. Did Teer get there okay?"

"He's here." She lowered her voice. "What's this all about? What does it have to do with you?"

Bruce hesitated, not sure how much to say. "I was worried about him. Heard where he might be. He rescued me when a big-ass branch fell on me and broke my arm. Don't ask where he was, Molly. Please. He doesn't want to talk about it."

"Little Teer rescued you? Well, that's...different."

"He's freaking amazing. If you're looking for him, though, you'll have to call here. He's staying with me for now."

Molly was quiet so long, he wondered if he'd made a mistake. "Is he? Huh. And you said 'please.' They'll be sending skis to hell this year."

"Hilarious."

"Just be nice to him, Bering, or I'll come break your other arm." Molly hesitated, then asked, "So are you two a thing now?"

"I don't know what we are. All I know is he needs someone right now."

"Don't kid yourself. So do you."

"Maybe." *Yeah.* Bruce cleared his throat. "So just remind him to get on the right bus after shift."

Molly laughed and reassured him she would before she hung up. He'd almost asked to talk to Teer, but lost his nerve. It would have been weird, Teer would just have been puzzled, and he didn't have any real reason to. *I just wanted to hear his voice, and isn't that just fucking bizarre.*

Later that morning, two of the guys from work brought Bruce's truck home for him. He thought about driving to the store, but thought maybe he'd put it off until Teer could come with him. The general really needed some supermarket experience. Instead, he did something he hadn't for months. He struggled one-armed to dig the Crock-Pot out of the cabinet and started a roast for dinner, the roast he'd bought the week before thinking about how hungry Teer might be if he turned up somewhere.

Teer let himself in a little after five, his heels clicking on the hardwood. "Bruce?"

"In here!" Bruce called from the kitchen where he had managed to chop up carrots for the Crock-Pot by using his right elbow to hold them down.

Teer stopped in the doorway, eyes closed as he inhaled deeply. "Oh, that smells wonderful."

"You better eat it. I don't care what kind of crap you ate while you were out in the woods."

"I had a bird. It was less than satisfying." Teer tossed his hair back, his earrings jingling. "Bruce, you don't have colored lights for this Christmas festival?"

Something twinged in Bruce's chest, but he ignored it and shrugged. "Haven't bothered the last couple years. What brought this on?"

"All of your neighbors have decorated their houses or trees *inside* their houses with lights. Don't you celebrate the anniversary of the sky-god's human avatar's birth?"

"I don't believe in all the religion mumbo-jumbo, but yeah, I used to. It's more tradition, I guess."

"Is there shame or censure attached to not observing these traditions?"

Bruce gaped at him before shaking his head. "The things you come up with. No, not really. It's nobody's business if I don't."

"You fear you will fail with the patience test of unknotting the lights. I'll help you. I helped Molly, so I assume it's not meant to be a solitary activity."

"Persistent little twerp, aren't you?" Bruce pointed to the kitchen table. "Not now. Sit down. Dinner."

Teer gazed up at him, unblinking. "Perhaps I'll carry dinner to the table since I have two hands."

"Fine," Bruce growled, bristling over being half-helpless, but he directed Teer to where the big platter was for the roast and how to safely remove it.

When they sat down to eat, Bruce with his huge slab and Teer with his child-sized portion, Teer picked up knife and fork in his gloved hands. These were black with delicate lavender diamonds running down each finger. *Where does he find this stuff?*

"Hey. It's just us. You don't have to keep your gloves on." Bruce shrugged, trying to muster disinterest he didn't feel. "Or anything else you don't want to wear."

Slowly, Teer set down his utensils. "You won't be offended? Or repulsed?"

"Seriously? You were naked when you carried me to the plane and you think I'll have a problem if you take your gloves off?"

"We weren't eating then."

"Christ on crackerjack, you're so damn weird." Bruce pointed with this fork. "Take the gloves off. Take everything off you feel like. I turned the heat down, but you're probably still too hot. We're guys, Teer. We get to sit around the house in our underwear if we damn well please unless we're having company."

Teer pulled the gloves off one finger at a time, dainty and precise as he was with everything. Anyone else, Bruce would've been irritated, but with Teer it wasn't an affectation. He was just being Teer, though he did take it a step farther than Bruce had expected. After the gloves, the high-heeled lavender boots came off, followed by the socks and the purple diamond-print shirt, all folded neatly and placed on the extra chair.

"Better?"

"Yes. Thank you."

The roast tasted better than any food had in a long time, and with Teer's soft, reasonable conversation to keep him company, Bruce couldn't find it strange at all to be having dinner with a half-naked alien.

Teer found comfort and regained his balance in routine and companionship. While Bruce was abrupt and coarse by Irasolan standards, he was brave, concerned about others, and more intelligent than his rough exterior implied. Every morning, Teer sat and watched the morning news with Bruce while the big human had his coffee and breakfast. Information-wise, the mornings were priceless, since now he no longer had to guess about human reactions and motives. Every night, he helped Bruce get ready for bed and then went to sleep on the wonderful bare wood floor in the guest room. It was the best sleep he'd managed in weeks.

Several days after he had taken up residence in Bruce's sizeable den, he returned from work to find the kitchen dark. This was unusual, since Bruce had always greeted him there before. Following Bruce's musk and soap scent led Teer to the basement door where cursing and irritated invective floated up the stairs.

"Bruce?" Teer hurried to shed his boots and gloves before he bounded down the stairs. "Are you all right?"

"Damn motherfucking box!" Bruce snarled and kicked out at the offending container. He cradled his broken arm, eyes squeezed shut in obvious pain.

"Bruce," Teer murmured and stroked his shoulder. "Have you done damage? Should I call for help?"

"No, damn it. Just...no." Bruce's words squeezed out, tight and miserable. Tears glinted on his cheeks, and he knew Bruce well enough to know those weren't from the pain.

The box that had fallen had two words printed on the top: *Mike* and *Christmas*. As carefully as possible, Teer righted the box and set it to the side. "Which box did you wish to take down?"

"It doesn't matter." Bruce collapsed on the bottom step with his head on his knees. "Oh...fuck. It doesn't matter."

Softly, so softly that Teer was certain he wasn't meant to hear, Bruce was weeping. Humans did this under extreme stress, he knew that, in most cases the circumstances mirroring the Irasolan need to howl. Mike had been Bruce's *arn*, his chosen life companion. The precipitous fall of that particular box had most likely triggered frustration and pain held close for too long. He risked Bruce's anger and sat beside him on the step, slowly sliding an arm across his shoulders.

Bruce shocked him by turning and burying his face in Teer's lap as his sorrow overwhelmed him, wracking choking sounds issuing from deep inside him, as if pulled from the marrow of his bones. Teer had seen humans comfort each other in such moments and he tried his best to imitate them, wrapping his arms tight around Bruce and rocking slowly with him, making little *shh shh* sounds.

Finally, Bruce sat back, wiping at his eyes. His voice was much calmer, but had a dull weariness to it. "Sorry. Didn't mean to blubber all over you."

"Perhaps it was necessary." Teer still stroked his good arm. "Now, what can I help you retrieve from this level?"

"There should be—" Bruce pulled in a shuddering breath and pointed with his chin. "—a box on top of that pile labeled *Lights*."

"I see it." Teer stood on tiptoe and pulled the box down without further mishap, then took Bruce by the arm and helped him upstairs. "Have you neglected to make dinner for yourself?"

"Was just gonna heat up some leftovers since this is a not-eating night for you."

Teer nodded and set the box down in the front hall. "I would suggest you do that while I begin the process of unknotting the lights. Are these meant for the inside or the outside?"

"Inside. Not really big on the idea of breaking my other arm falling off the roof."

Good. Bruce's usual growling tone had returned. Opening and closing of drawers and doors and the rattling of plates and utensils came from the kitchen, so Teer felt comfortable leaving Bruce on his own. He knelt on the floor by the box, of that thick paper humans called *cardboard*, and carefully lifted out strands of glass bulbs. As Molly had shown him, he plugged the strands in one by one to see which ones were operational.

Unfortunately, while the spot he chose to work had plenty of space for untangling, it was too close to a heat vent. While he freed and carefully coiled three strands, he shed clothing like a *var* shed skins until he was dressed in only the pelt he had from hatching.

Teer picked his head up at a change in sounds. The kitchen noises had ceased. He padded around the corner and found Bruce leaning against the sink, draining water from a bowl of something that smelled vegetative. The broad, strong back, the muscular backside shouldn't have excited him. Bruce was the opposite of everything he had ever found attractive. Either living among human attitudes had begun to change him, or his body recognized as attractive someone he admired, regardless of body type.

Though that last thought seemed far too noble as his sac and cock breached, parting their slit with painful haste. He had no idea how his advances would be received, but his hand reached out to stroke Bruce's side before he could order a halt. Purring softly, he pressed up against Bruce's back.

"Hey...hi." Bruce turned into Teer's arms, a hint of a smile on his lips. "I don't know if I can—you're naked. Well, as naked as you get."

"I apologize for the suddenness. You simply looked so inviting there." Teer licked his lips, gazing up into eyes the shade of life. "Please tell me no if you have no de—"

A mortifying squeak escaped him when Bruce cut off his words by clamping his lips down on Teer's. Of course, he had seen humans kiss, but the actual sensation was strange, not unpleasant, just different from anything he knew. *Incredibly different.* Bruce's lips began to move against his in soft caresses. *Amazingly different.*

Teer caressed back and found it more than pleasant. It was enough to cause full descent and a pleasured ache in his *lunamon*. He pulled back, toying with the buttons of Bruce's shirt. "I don't wish to cause you pain. You should be made comfortable somewhere."

Bruce smoothed Teer's mane back from his forehead, his gaze traveling slowly up and down Teer's body. "Huh. You do have the whole package." He had the audacity to swat Teer's hip. "Go upstairs. I'll meet you there. Let me get a couple bites of dinner down over the pain meds."

Unused to taking orders during sex, Teer simply stared at him for a few heartbeats. But he wasn't home, Bruce wasn't Irasolan, and his body was screaming at him to put his ego away. "I'll be upstairs," he murmured softly and did his best to mount a dignified retreat.

Bruce guzzled a whole glass of water to try to slow his panting. Kissing Teer had been about the hottest thing he'd experienced in years. Not since...

Damn it, Mike. Why'd you have to leave me? Everything I own, everything I do has your ghost fingers in it. I feel guilty just looking. I feel guilty when I laugh.

I feel guilty just being here with you gone.

He gripped the counter with his good arm, the tears threatening again. Here he was thinking Teer was the one in danger of falling apart. Teer was fine. *He* was a damn mess.

So what's the problem? Mike said in his head, big as life, with that goofy, friendly smile he always had.

He's not you. I feel like I'm cheating on you.

I'm dead, dumbass.

I know that. Mike, I still miss you so bad. It hurts so much.

Doesn't make you less of a dumbass, Bering. You really think I'd want you miserable like this? You think it was about ownership? I loved you, asshole. So you honor my memory by not living?

Mike—

Live, damn you! How fucked up is your head that you think falling for someone new is cheating on a dead man?

Falling for—? Is that what I'm doing?

But Mike was gone, the strange subconscious visit over. Bruce wolfed down some of the peas and the frozen lasagna he'd nuked, swallowing hard past a tight throat. Was it that simple? Was he just being a dumbass?

Maybe. He trudged up the stairs, still turning things over and over, and found Teer sitting cross-legged on his comforter, his black fur beautiful against the burgundy. Head up, spine straight, Teer reminded Bruce of paintings of emperors and shoguns. This was a person who had been important in his old life, maybe even famous, someone who held lives in his hands, who was accustomed to command. All of Bruce's misgivings about bestiality melted under that calm, thoughtful gaze. Sure, the construction was different, but Teer was a reasoning, thinking person who deserved respect, not some exotic animal.

"Bruce?"

Obviously he'd been staring too long. "Hey. So, how do you want to do this? I don't—" Bruce ran a hand back through his hair. "I don't want to do something wrong."

Teer patted the comforter. "There is no wrong. I'll tell you if something hurts and you must do the same. Let me help you with the shirt."

At least this part was familiar since Teer had been helping him with his shirt buttons since he came to stay. Bruce sat down on the bed and sat still for Teer, swallowing hard when Teer's fingers brushed a nipple on the way down.

"I want to see all of you." Teer petted his chest hair. "I had thought humans without body hair until I saw yours. Is it common?"

"Most have body hair. Not as much as me." Bruce stood to undo his jeans. He shoved them down and stepped out so he was standing in front of Teer in only his boxer briefs. "A lot of guys you see on TV manscape, um, depilate. Women have body hair, too, but less, and a lot shave their legs."

Teer made that sexy purring sound as he hooked two fingers in the briefs and pulled them down to Bruce's knees. "Your beautiful golden pelt doesn't extend everywhere, but it's quite thick in spots."

"Mmm," Bruce managed as Teer's hair brushed over his cock, which was quickly taking a stand to show its appreciation. He ran a hand through the thick mane to push Teer back gently. "Why is yours everywhere except your face and neck?"

Teer turned his head to nuzzle Bruce's palm. "I suppose it is a reproductive adaptation. The skin of our faces is so sensitive, the fine down rather than full pelt heightens the pleasure. One does *not* touch another's face except during intimacy and to go about with one's face exposed is considered obscene."

"Well, crap." Bruce shimmied out of the briefs and sat down beside Teer. "We must've seemed really rude."

"It took some adjustment," Teer said in his dry way. He reached up to stroke Bruce's short-cropped hair. "Would your mane—your hair be the same gold as your chest if you allowed it to grow?"

"A little lighter." He shivered as Teer stroked his back carefully with a claw tip. Maybe he'd let his hair grow out again. "Was the kiss rude? Damn, I'm sorry."

"Ha. No. It was exciting. Intimate, Bruce. In public, I would balk." Teer hesitated, frowning at the bed. "Is this done on top of the blankets?"

Bruce could have kicked himself. This was unfamiliar territory for both of them. He took Teer's hand, warm tingling spreading through his belly when furred fingers closed tight around his. "On top's fine. Come on. Lie down with me."

Teer prowled up the bed to stretch out and held his arms out in invitation. With Bruce's cock shouting a hallelujah, he made his way up the bed with a lot less grace but enough determination for both of them. Careful to keep his broken arm on top, he nudged in close with his head on Teer's soft-furred shoulder. It should've felt weird. Instead, it felt comfortable and, yes, if he was honest, comforting. Thoughts of perversion tried to wriggle back in, but he shoved them out and plugged up the holes.

The softest fur was at the joints and Teer squirmed, purring louder when Bruce stroked at the bend of his thigh. "Ticklish?"

"A bit. It feels so good, though. Touch. Wherever you please." Teer backed up his words with action, dragging his padded hand down Bruce's side to stroke his hip and thigh. Bruce's breath hitched when Teer palmed his ass, and the furred hand froze. "Good or bad?"

"Good. Definitely good." Bruce arched back into the touch when Teer started kneading, claws pricking delicately at his skin. "So damn good."

Frustrated by his clumsiness with one immobilized arm, Bruce sat up to run his fingers through Teer's chest fur in long strokes. He cupped the slit where a human's bellybutton would've been, biting his bottom lip as Teer arched and moaned.

"You liked other guys before you came here, right?"

"Yes." Teer slid a hand up his thigh and cupped Bruce's sac, pulling out a matching pleasured moan. "It is usual. Normal."

"Lucky you," Bruce grumbled and moved his hand to Teer's hip. "With other guys, other males, is it normal to penetrate your...L-word thing? I don't remember the name."

"*Lunamon*. Yes." Now Teer sat up as well to make a more thorough examination of Bruce's erection. "Yours is longer than the ones I'm accustomed to, but not much more in diameter."

They looked up in unison, and Bruce hoped the intensity in Teer's eyes was molten desire. "You'd need to be on top. Me with one arm and all."

Teer moved suddenly and decisively, shoving Bruce onto his back and climbing on top to straddle his hips. "The placement of things is not so different. But let me lead. I'm uncertain whether it will accept your naked skin."

"Do you need...I mean...condoms, probably not, right? But lube?"

"You and I are healthy and I have doubts that human illnesses could jump species." Teer leaned down to lick Bruce's ear, a sensual slide around the outer edge. "Lube? Lubricant? No need. I'm young enough and aroused enough to have my own."

Bruce didn't have time to process that thought since Teer's hand closed around his cock, stroking gently. He gasped and tried not to squirm as Teer scooted down to position himself. The fur against Bruce's cock head was decadent and incredible. He clenched the comforter hard to keep himself from thrusting up.

"Gently, gently." Teer pressed down, a warm, wet heat enveloping Bruce, slick and tight as Teer slid down on him. "Bruce, breathe, please. Is it all right?"

Bruce let out his breath on a strangled laugh. "Hell, yes. It's so much better than all right, I think my brain just melted." He smoothed the fur on Teer's hip. "You?"

"Yes. Oh...yes," Teer whispered as he sank down farther, dragging moans from them both. "Can you reach me? Touch me?"

It took a second to figure out what Teer meant and then another to figure out how to manage it. With Bruce's cock impaling Teer where a human bellybutton would be, he couldn't reach Teer's cock, no matter how he bent or stretched. He grunted in frustration since he couldn't lever himself up on his broken arm. Inspiration struck, and Bruce parted his legs far enough to take Teer's furry erection between his almost-as-furry thighs, closing them so Teer could thrust between them.

Breathing in little sips, Teer buried his face against Bruce's chest and started to move, shoving his cock up and down within the tight embrace of Bruce's thighs, while pumping Bruce's hard length in and out of his brood pouch.

"What do you need?" Teer asked in an urgent whisper. "How do I please you?"

"You're doing it. Don't worry," Bruce panted out as the constriction on his cock increased with every pump of Teer's body. "Oh God...yes."

Teer's purring started to mix with little chirps and growls. His body's undulations sped up, taking Bruce in almost to his base. "I can't...Bruce...I'm sorry."

"Go on." Bruce wrapped his good arm hard around Teer and rolled his hips gently, the squeezing on his cock making his eyes cross. "It's all right, Teer. Let go. I've got you."

Teer lifted his head, his eyes wide open and glassy.

His body clamped hard around Bruce. He threw back his head and howled. It was unlike anything Bruce had ever heard, a strange, eerie music that vibrated through his bones. He didn't have many brain cells to spare, though, since Teer's *lunamon* clenched and released hard around him and Teer's cock splashed hot jets on his legs. Dark spots obscuring parts of his vision, he cried out and came hard, every fierce pulse making him buck and jerk.

With a whimper, Teer pulled off and crawled to the other side of the bed where he stayed on all fours, head hanging, breathing in whistling gasps.

"Teer? Hey, hey..." Bruce rolled over, unsure whether to touch or to leave him alone. "Did I hurt you?"

Apparently still trying to get his breath back, Teer shook his head and held up a finger. Finally, he gasped out, "No...no. That was... It was...it was nearly too much. I've never...just never."

Bruce reached out to stroke Teer's shoulder. The muscle under his hand flinched, but Teer didn't pull away. "Come lie down?"

"In a moment. Everything is still leaping and dancing." Teer laughed, a breathy, throaty sound Bruce hadn't heard from him. "Your semen apparently heightens the orgasm. It still tingles inside."

"Huh. Like those warming lubes, kind of. I guess. You sure you're okay?"

"I'm well. I am." Teer crawled back to him and sprawled out beside him, petting his chest. "I will be a bit sore since I rushed things, but that was astounding."

"You were pretty amazing too." Bruce settled Teer's head on his shoulder. "Guess you can't sleep here with me, huh?"

"I'm sorry. Your bed is too soft."

"And yours is too hard. Like the three bears."

"Which bears are those?"

"Kid's story. I'll tell you later. Stay for a little while?"

Teer nuzzled at Bruce's throat with one of those low, rumbling growls, the one Bruce had decided was a happy sound. His general stayed with him until he'd fallen asleep.

TWO DAYS LATER, THEY HAD FOUND APPROPRIATE places for all the working lights. Bruce had said that the nonworking strands could be reactivated but it was "too much of a pain." A multicolored strand ran around the large glass doors beside the kitchen table where Teer sat with his tablet looking through advertisements for apartment rentals. It would be better, he'd decided, to find one nearer Bruce's house. That way he would be nearby if Bruce needed him, something in walking distance so they could see each other regularly.

With a harrumph, Bruce set a glass beside him, went back to the kitchen to retrieve another for himself, and sat down across the table.

"What did that noise mean?" Teer picked up the glass and sniffed its contents. Milk and...something. "And what's this?"

"It's milk and amaretto. Just try it." Bruce sipped from his own glass, a clear, golden liquid that smelled vile.

With a last sniff, Teer tried a sip and let out an involuntary purr. "Delicious. Oh, I could drink bottles of this."

"Don't you even think about it."

"And the noise?"

Bruce frowned down at his drink. "You are staying through the holidays, right? You're not gonna spend it in that sorry, empty excuse for an apartment, are you?"

"If you need me, certainly. It doesn't seem possible to secure another apartment so quickly."

Bruce grumbled something into his drink that Teer didn't catch, but before he could ask, the bell at the front of the house announced a visitor. Teer froze. He wore only a pair of boxers with red hearts on them. The stairs, and the path to the rest of his clothes, stood in sight of the front door.

"Relax. Stay there." Bruce patted his hand and rose, palming his wallet from the counter on his way to the front hall.

While he knew it was unlikely that anyone would barge past Bruce and into his house, Teer still made note of all of his escape options. Basement door. Pantry. Out into the back garden. No, his fur would show too visibly against the snow.

"Oh great, thanks," Bruce said to the person at the door. "Yeah, right there on the front table's great. Appreciate it."

There were a few more sentences of polite conversation. Then the door closed and Teer slumped in relief, returning to his apartment search and his wonderful milk drink. It took him a moment to realize Bruce had returned to lean against the kitchen doorway with a worried frown.

"You're supposed to ask who was at the door."

"Oh." Teer blinked in surprise. There were always bits of human courtesy he seemed to be missing. "Who was at the door?"

"Delivery," Bruce said, which was either code for something or deliberately vague.

"Oh?"

"Look, I—" Bruce rubbed his good hand over the back of his neck. "I did something I'm not sure about. Maybe I should've asked you, since I don't want you to be uncomfortable or get mad at me."

Teer set his tablet down carefully. "I won't be angry over a misunderstanding. I can't promise not to be uncomfortable. Perhaps you should tell me."

Bruce held out his hand. "C'mere. I'll show you."

Curious, Teer finished his drink and took the offered hand, following Bruce out into the hall. His breath caught when he saw the two *alna*, one with yellow blooms.

"I know it's a couple days still, but they're an early Christmas present."

"For whom?"

"For you, you twerp. Who else would they be for?"

"Oh." Teer stared at them, unable to form a coherent thought. "Bruce...I can't."

Bruce's frown deepened. "You can't what? Can't accept presents? Can't accept them from me?"

Teer sat on the bottom step with his head in his

hands, trying to control his chirps of distress. "It's too much."

"Like hell it is. They weren't expensive."

"Plants are sacred. Precious." Teer flexed his claws, trying to find some calm from the bits of pain along his scalp. "I can't *own* one. Certainly not one that looks like...*alna*."

"I thought you liked them." Bruce sat beside him, making the stair creak. "You think they're ugly?"

"No. They're beautiful. They look like something from home." A yelp escaped Teer, the beginning of a howl bitten off hard. "I'm too damaged, too dishonored for something like that."

Bruce pulled him into a fierce, one-armed hug. "Look at us. Holding onto the past so hard it's like we're stuck in amber. Maybe it's time you told me what you did, General."

Teer transferred both hands to the front of Bruce's shirt, clinging to his warmth, needing to feel the beat of that strong, generous heart. "General Teer of the Seventh Horath, hero of the Violet Day Offensive. My full title. We...have been at war, on and off, with the Fara for generations."

"The Fara? Are they like you?"

Teer shook his head against Bruce's shoulder. "No and yes. They are more like your crustaceans in appearance. But they are spacefarers like us. We disagree on...many things. I had the heir to the Keerop training with me. Karet's son. I swore to his father that I would keep the boy safe. Our intelligence was faulty. The Fara attacked my Horath. The boy, Tinth, wished to fight, to prove himself. He disabled one of my pilots. Stole a fighter. I realized too late, and though I moved to protect him, the boy died."

Bruce stroked his shoulder gently, but his tone bristled as he asked, "So some punk-ass royal brat does whatever the hell he pleases and gets himself killed and they blame *you*?"

"I broke my oath. Don't you see? I had sworn to protect him. It is—was my duty, my purpose, to protect. I thought my past service might allow me an honorable execution, but my disgrace was too great." Teer couldn't help himself any longer, a small howl escaped.

"Okay, I get that. The whole protect-and-serve thing." Bruce held him tighter, as if to shield him from the memories. "I get that you feel like you failed. Still think it's a shitty thing to do, to blame you for someone else's stupidity."

He set Teer back, searching his face, and smoothed his mane back from his forehead. Gently, he kissed Teer's cheek, a gesture both intimate and tender.

"Guess what, though? You're not there. You're here. And those aren't *alna* plants. Nothing sacred or really that special about them. They're just pretty Earth plants that you happened to like. And guess what else? I think you're worth it. That you deserve them."

Teer pulled in a hissing breath, trying to ease the suffocating weight on his chest. "That's...kind of you. But even from a practical standpoint, I can't keep them. My apartment has so little light. They will die. And who knows what my new apartment will be like?"

"See, about that." Bruce chewed on his bottom lip,

an oddly sensual gesture to indicate uncertainty. "I was hoping I could talk you into staying. So, um, the plants are kind of a bribe too."

"But I've said I would stay through the holidays." Teer searched his face, puzzled.

"Yeah. I mean stay to stay, though. Move in with me. Live here with me." Bruce looked away, swallowing hard. "I really like having you around. Even if we can't sleep in the same bed, it's...it's like this screaming thing that's lived inside me for two years finally shut up since you've been here."

Teer sat back to lean against the banister posts, though he kept a firm hold on Bruce's hand. "You want me to cohabitate with you? As a more...permanent arrangement? Is it merely comfort or does this have some significance I'm missing?"

"It means whatever we damn well want it to mean," Bruce growled, his voice rising. Then he shook his head, apparently trying for a softer tone. "Yeah, some people would read into it. Say we're a couple. That I'm your boyfriend. You get that concept, right?"

Bruce seemed to be waiting for Teer, so he nodded. Yes, he understood the courting significance of *boyfriend*.

"Okay. That's fine. They can think whatever they want. But I've thought about this a lot this week. I like you. More than like you. You're something really special..." Bruce let out a helpless laugh. "Of course you are. There's no one like you on Earth. I like knowing that you're coming home to me at night. I like having you across from me at breakfast. I like everything with you—talking, sex, movies, driving to the damn store. It's like...like the color's put back in everything when you're around."

"Does this lead to a more serious attachment?"

"Sometimes. Yeah. I'd never pressure you."

Teer stroked the back of Bruce's hand, rough-knuckled and oversized. He was human, without even a hint of the deadly grace of an Irasolan male. His voice was loud. His speech often crude. He ate as if there would be no more food left tomorrow, and he carried a dead man's weight with him wherever he went.

So much Teer should have found distasteful but didn't. He liked Bruce, found comfort in him, had found a need in himself to protect him. Could he do this without guilt? Accept peace, comfort, and someone to fill the howling void?

"Teer?"

"Yes."

"Yes to what? You'll stay or you'll accept the present?"

"Both." Teer placed his hands on either side of Bruce's face and leaned in to place a soft kiss on his lips. Humans did these things and it wasn't always sexual. "I will stop my search for an apartment nearby and stay with you. And I thank you for the cacti. If I am here, they belong to both of us."

Bruce crushed him close, hot droplets falling onto Teer's shoulder, but somehow he thought they were relief rather than anguish.

To Bruce's surprise, Teer decided he was taking over Christmas. He'd anticipated a nice, leisurely day with the two of them at home, no work, no obligations, but Teer had other ideas.

At breakfast, he'd presented Bruce with a new pair of gloves since his right one was all scuffed and torn after the pine branch incident. He suspected Molly's hand in that and Teer seemed happier to be able to reciprocate the gift giving. Then he insisted they were going to the cemetery.

"It's not Friday."

"No. It's a holiday."

"I kinda just wanted to spend the day with you."

"You will."

Teer just stared at him with that unshakeable patience of his and Bruce finally agreed, grumbling all the way through getting dressed.

"So you're dragging my broken-armed ass out into the cold, why, exactly?" Bruce growled as he started up the truck. It was a pain to drive one-armed, but manageable.

"We're visiting Mike. I'd like a word with him."

That shut Bruce up. He shot Teer anxious sideways glances as they drove, trying to figure out what was going on in Teer's lovely head. Some days, he was getting good at it, others, not so much. Sex, at least, had been amazing as they discovered the secrets of each other's bodies, from sensitive spots to possibilities for getting each other off. Bruce even found he could give Teer a blowjob if he stayed at the smooth head and didn't venture too far into the fur zone. Too hard to keep up the suction with the fuzz. Teer's handjobs, though, were amazing with those rough pads and the occasional pricking of careful claws.

Bruce pulled up to the cemetery entrance on Fairbanks and turned in to park. He'd made sure that Teer had sensible boots on before they left the house and a jacket, since being out here in ten degrees without one would just look too strange. Teer scrambled out of the truck and retrieved something from behind the seat.

"What's that?" Bruce shoved his good hand in his pocket and nodded to the bundle.

"For Mike." Teer unwrapped the plastic from the top of the bundle to reveal a dozen scarlet roses.

"I don't bring him roses," Bruce growled. "One purple hyacinth. Every Friday."

"Yes. I don't wish to interfere with your usual routines, but I have been researching the meanings of Earth flowers. Purple is for sorrow. Red is for love. For that one love you choose above others."

Bruce opened his mouth and lost what he was going to say. The words tumbled out and lay stupid and stunned in the snow. Shaking his head, he led the way into the cemetery, heading unerringly toward Mike's grave. Teer followed, his head swiveling back and forth as he took it all in.

"This is a beautiful place." Teer tucked his free hand into the crook of Bruce's arm. The gloves today were red leather, for Christmas, probably.

"Nicer in the spring with everything blooming. You probably don't bury your dead and you think we're bizarre."

"We don't. Difficult to bury anything in frozen ground."

"Right."

"My ancestors used to eat their dead. The whole community was involved, a little piece given to everyone."

"Oh, gross."

"Hmm. Perhaps. Efficient use of resources. We no longer do this. The body is given to scavengers. But we do have memorials not so different from this."

They arrived at Mike's grave without meeting another soul, pretty much expected on Christmas morning. Bruce knelt down carefully and brushed the snow from the marker.

"Hey, Bowser. I know I'm off schedule, but someone wanted to come see you."

Teer knelt beside him and offered him the bundle of roses.

"Oh, yeah. And we brought you something kinda special, 'cause it's Christmas." Taking great care not to cover up Mike's name, Bruce set the bundle of roses on the marker.

Teer patted his knee and began to speak. "Hello, Mike, and Happy Christmas. My name is Teer. Though we've never met, I feel as though I know you from stories Bruce has told and from all the things of yours in the house. I live with Bruce now, you see, and it's more than evident that he still loves you desperately."

A breath caught in Bruce's throat. *I'm not gonna start bawling now. Hell, no.*

"So I thought it best to come speak with you. Bruce has been suffering since you died. That's understandable. But when he met me, I think he recognized someone else suffering. I was so terribly alone and hanging onto sanity by a thread." Teer took Bruce's hand in both of his to hold in his lap. "He was kind to me and came to find me when I was lost. I owe him my life, but this is more than gratitude, what lies between us. He will always love you. We need to both acknowledge that. But he mustn't forget to live because of loving you."

Bruce bit down on his bottom lip, squeezing his eyes shut against the sting of tears.

"I will never seek to replace you. But I came to make you a promise. I will do my best to see that Bruce lives. That he takes joy in life again. Purple is for sorrow. Perhaps it's time he put the sorrow to the side and come see you in memory of the love you had for him, instead."

Bruce managed to keep it to a single, chest-aching sob, but it was a close thing. Bruce took his hand back to trace the *M* of Mike's name before he bothered to wipe the freezing tears away.

"Merry Christmas, Mike," Bruce whispered and Teer sat silently beside him, shoulder to shoulder, letting him take all the time he needed.

Finally, he got up, with Teer helping discreetly, and began the trudge back to the car. Behind him, he heard Teer whisper, "I'll take care of him, Mike. I promise."

The sun glinted diamonds off his frozen lashes. Somehow, instead of causing him pain, the new tears felt bright and clean.

THE *ALNA*—NO, THE CHRISTMAS CACTI HAD THEIR own table beside the glass doors where Teer could see them every morning and where they would receive the most sun. He still set up an artificial light for them. The days had grown short and the sunlight scarce.

He sat beside Bruce after their Christmas dinner of turkey and noodles, holding his hand and watching the snowfall while Bruce sipped his whiskey and Teer his eggnog. Eggnog was delicious, and Bruce had bought the kind without the alcohol added, but he had to be careful of his milk intake. It was his second glass and he didn't want stomach cramps ruining the evening.

"You're really staying?"

"I'm staying. Tomorrow, I will go to the office at the apartment building and tell them I no longer need the space. I may have to pay for the remainder of the contract, but I'm willing to. I'll bring the rest of my clothes then."

Bruce squeezed his hand and sipped. "We can look at those Sleep Number beds if you want, you know. Or get a board for your half of the bed."

"I would appreciate that. I'm always sad to leave you when you fall asleep."

"Well, good." Bruce picked up his hand and kissed the backs of his fingers. "Thank you. For staying. For understanding...everything."

"I could say the same." Teer slid his chair closer so he could lean his head on Bruce's shoulder. It would be good when the cast came off and Bruce could use both arms again.

The yellow and salmon blossoms looked so beautiful against the snowy backdrop. Such a perfect, handsome combination of colors. Teer frowned at the drab gray on either side of the doors.

"Bruce? I'm wondering if you'd consider some new curtains."

The End

The Nut Job
Freddy MacKay

ALSO BY ANGEL MARTINEZ

BRANDYWINE INVESTIGATIONS

Brandywine Investigations: Open for Business (Omnibus)

Brandywine Investigations: Family Matters (Omnibus)

BRIMSTONE

Potato Surprise #1

Hell for the Company #2

Fear of Frogs #3

Shax's War #4

Beside a Black Tarn #5

The Brimstone Journals: Collection One

The Brimstone Journals: Collection Two

The Hunt for Red Fluffy #6

The Brimstone Journals: Collection Three

A Fine Mess #7

THE ENDANGERED FAE SERIES

Finn

Diego

Semper Fae

No Fae is an Island

ESTO UNIVERSE

Vassily the Beautiful

Prisoner 374215

A Matter of Faces

Gravitational Attraction

Sub Zero

LIJUN Trilogy (with Freddy Mackay)

Fireworks & Stolen Kisses

Trysts & Burning Embers

Detonations & Devotion (TBD)

INTERPLANETARY MULTISPECIES PACT (IMP)

A Christmas Cactus for the General

A Message from the Home Office

PUDDING PROTOCOLS UNIVERSE

Safety Protocols for Human Holidays

The Solstice Pudding

THE WEB OF ARCANA

The Mage on the Hill

OFFBEAT CRIMES

Lime Gelatin and Other Monsters

Pill Bugs of Time

Skim Blood & Savage Verse

Feral Dust Bunnies

Jackalopes & Woofen-Poofs

All the World's an Undead Stage

SINGLE TITLES

Eating Stars

Yule Planet

The Color of His Crest

Hearts & Flowers: A Tale of Hay Fever and Bad Decor

Boots

The Line

AURA UNIVERSE (with Bellora Quinn)

Quinn's Gambit

Flax's Pursuit

Kellen's Awakening

9 798664 371789